CAPTAIN NI'MAT'S LAST BATTLE

CAPTAIN NI'MAT'S
Last Battle

Mohamed Leftah

Translated from the French by Lara Vergnaud

OTHER PRESS
NEW YORK

Originally published in French as *Le dernier combat du captain Ni'mat*
in 2011 by Éditions de la Différence, Paris, and reprinted
in 2020 by La Croisée des chemins, Casablanca
Copyright © Éditions La Croisée des Chemins, 2011
Published by arrangement with
Agence littéraire Astier-Pécher

English translation copyright © Lara Vergnaud, 2022

Epigraphs by Charles Baudelaire from *The Flowers of Evil*,
translated by James McGowan, Oxford University Press, 1993.
Translation and Notes © James McGowan 1993. Reproduced
with permission of the Licensor through PLSclear.

Production editor: Yvonne E. Cárdenas
Text designer: Jennifer Daddio / Bookmark Design & Media Inc.
This book was set in Cochin by
Alpha Design & Composition of Pittsfield, NH

1 3 5 7 9 10 8 6 4 2

Library of Congress Cataloging-in-Publication Data
Names: Leftah, Mohamed, author. | Vergnaud, Lara, translator.
Title: Captain Ni'mat's last battle / Mohamed Leftah ; translated from
the French by Lara Vergnaud.
Other titles: Dernier combat du captain Ni'mat. English
Description: New York : Other Press, [2022] | Originally published
in French as Le dernier combat du captain Ni'mat in 2011
by Éditions de la Différence, Paris, and reprinted in 2020
by La Croisée des chemins, Casablanca.
Identifiers: LCCN 2021051201 (print) | LCCN 2021051202 (ebook) |
ISBN 9781635420647 (paperback) | ISBN 9781635420654 (ebook)
Subjects: LCGFT: Gay fiction. | Novels.
Classification: LCC PQ3989.2.L427 D4713 2022 (print) |
LCC PQ3989.2.L427 (ebook) | DDC 843/.92—dc23/eng/20220131
LC record available at https://lccn.loc.gov/2021051201
LC ebook record available at https://lccn.loc.gov/2021051202

Publisher's Note
This is a work of fiction. Names, characters, places, and
incidents either are the product of the author's imagination
or are used fictitiously, and any resemblance to actual persons,
living or dead, events, or locales is entirely coincidental.

I

Undecidable Beauty

What difference, then, from heaven or from hell,

O Beauty, monstrous in simplicity?

If eye, smile, step can open me the way

To find unknown, sublime infinity?

BAUDELAIRE, "HYMN TO BEAUTY"

1

FROM THE START of that sweltering month of August, the adults-only swimming pool at the Ma'adi club had transformed into the theater for a new, niggling, and cruel confrontation. With their own pool undergoing renovations, the boys on the club's youth swim team now went there to practice every early afternoon.

As soon as the adults, mostly of retirement age, heard the swell of youthful voices, the shouting and laughter, and even before their hitherto peaceful and hushed world was overrun, they started to exit the pool in succession, like soldiers of an army defeated even before it has waged battle.

All that then remained of the water was a still, flat, and silent surface, as if in wait. The young invaders, after putting on their swimsuits in the changing room, would take a running start and dive in like swordfish, ripping this shimmering blue dress down the middle and adorning it with white foam.

Then the pool, in motion again, alive, churned and furrowed in every direction by flesh, some as white and delicate as halibut, would start to resemble a miniature sea. Better: the original, primordial sea, when early, trembling life first began to twitch and take form, so fragile then but already fated for a splendor and lushness such that over time, geological eras, it would spread across the entire globe.

To the adults who returned to dry land, relinquishing the aquatic element to the young bodies who slipped into the water, moving with magnificent ease, this mismatched confrontation didn't appear to be merely the clash of two ages in life, but almost of two stages of evolution.

Captain Ni'mat, the audacious (or reckless) amphibian, hadn't regained shore, and found himself trapped in this sea from the dawn of time. Unable to swim amid the supple and wriggling bodies penning him in on all sides, he turned onto his back and quite simply tried to keep his own afloat, his stocky limbs obliged to make imperceptible, pseudopodic movements. The harsh glare of the August light, which to him seemed to emanate from the very bodies among which he was trapped, was blinding. He closed his eyes and let himself drift like floating algae.

Suddenly, he heard the nickname everyone called him by—"Captain Ni'mat!"—though he had been dismissed from the army years ago. His longtime friends, former companions in arms, were summoning him, and he could already hear the unvarying joke that would greet him once he emerged from the water: "You done slobbering over that school of wriggling sardines, you old seal?"

He had no desire to join his friends at their reserved table, beneath the pergola where bougainvillea was blooming in pink and white clusters.

When he attempted to flip onto his stomach, his hand brushed against a young swimmer's thigh. The crural skin was so shockingly soft that he felt like he'd received an electric jolt. In the same instant, the alternating, powerful kicking of two feet nearly in his face sent up violent jets of water and foam. The young swimmer was already far off, splitting the water like an arrow. His vocabulary, like that of his friends, undoubtedly didn't include the civilized "Pardon" that Captain Ni'mat and the men of his generation instinctively uttered when their bodies bumped, or merely grazed, that of another swimmer.

The captain finally made up his mind to leave the water. He swam, with difficulty, toward one of two metal ladders, the one closest to the pergola, internally cursing the club management that had the misguided idea of allowing their pool to be invaded by young barbarians. Before this intrusion, he had felt perfectly fine in his blubbery skin, dividing his afternoons, like his comrades, between quick dips in the water and an endless stream of joke-filled chatter, first in the warmth of the sauna, then beneath the pergola, in the cool and soothing shade of the bougainvillea.

He emerged from the pool, the ladder's three or four rungs creaking and moaning beneath his weight, and stretched out on a lounger to dry off. He tried, in vain, to prevent fragments of his friends' discussion—if one can call the tireless regurgitation of the same comments and jokes a discussion—from seeping into his ears and successfully reaching his brain. Nonetheless, the name of a country, Yemen, breached the barrier, dragging in its wake thundering and wince-inducing bursts of laughter. The *liwa*, General Midhat, was no doubt telling, for the thousandth time, the story of the Egyptian MiG pilot who released a 450-pound bomb that flattened a mangy donkey, turning it into ground meat, as the Imam's Yemeni warriors chuckled away, safe in their caves, smoothing their beards and chewing on khat. On occasion the infantry had been able to capture one of these strange herbivorous warriors, a Kalashnikov over one shoulder and waist belted by grenades in the center of which shone precious stones inlaid in the sheath of a *khanjar*. The bastard's only response to the rough interrogation to which he would then be subjected was to merely point at his cheek, monstrously swollen by khat chewing, signifying by this gesture that he had a terrible abscess in his mouth that prevented him from speaking.

Suddenly, as if the ectoplasm of one of those warrior–khat chewers had materialized following *liwa* Midhat's tired anecdote, Captain Ni'mat felt a sharp bite on his cheek, which seemed to him to swell instantaneously. A wasp, a hymenopteran abundant in the outdoor complex where the pool had been dug, had burrowed into his skin and left its stinger behind.

Captain Ni'mat insulted and cursed the hymenopteran and its progeny to the fourth generation, the fly that arrived immediately after to take its place, and the crow that then landed, announcing the news to those that preceded it with a victorious and sinister caw. Good God, where were the wood pigeons?! The birds that long ago enchanted Cairo's rich blue sky, moving with such grace, had now practically deserted it. In what secret place could beauty still be found within this noisy, dirty metropolis whose inhabitants, though life was becoming increasingly difficult, still proudly and lovingly called it Umm al Dunya, "the mother of the universe"?

Captain Ni'mat cast an irate glance at his companions when they hailed him yet again. He truly had no desire to join them but knew that by the most powerful of tropisms, quite simply habit, he would eventually respond to their summons. They were past the inglorious episode of the Yemen expedition, which had nonetheless ended with the defeat of the Imam and the establishment of Egypt's sister republic, thanks to the military coup d'état of 1962. They had blithely skipped over the tragedy of June 1967, though *liwa* Behjat had tossed out a few well-chosen insults to the memory of the pharaoh, under whom they had served and endured a great loss. The men had now reached the most thrilling moment of their historical saga, the glorious, immortal victory of 1973 to which they referred, depending on the calendar used, as the October victory or the Ramadan victory, rendering it doubly immortal in a way.

Captain Ni'mat himself had always had a more measured and objective view of this glorious event. Taking into account the political evolution that followed, as well as, on the military side, the reverse crossing of the Suez Canal by Israeli troops that launched a rear attack on Egypt's Third Army, which found itself surrounded and remained so until the signing of the ceasefire, he felt that this immortal victory was in fact merely a modest victory, if not to say a partial one. But he never dared to express this opinion, as he hadn't participated in this war, having been expelled from the army a few months after the scathing defeat of 1967. The mass reorganization of the air force in the wake of that defeat weeded out not only incompetent officers but also those who had returned from the Yemen campaign, like him, with socialist or even Marxist leanings much more pronounced than those of the sole party in power at the time.

Both embarrassed by his nonparticipation in a war through which his former companions in arms, nearly all retired generals now, had erased the shame of 1967, and in no way wanting to become a pariah in their eyes, Captain Ni'mat had kept his thoughts to himself during all these years gone by.

After scratching his cheek for a while, he finally extracted with his thumb and index finger the hornet's stinger embedded in his skin. *Achwak al hayat!*—thorns of life—he gloomily thought, and in the same instant felt annoyance with this language, classical Arabic, whose emphatic set expressions came to mind and mouth without even being sought for, as if it had a mind of its own and was thinking on one's behalf. Thankfully, it (life) also has its roses. For Captain Ni'mat abruptly realized—this came to him like a revelation—that the beauty he had been pondering a few moments earlier, wondering in what secret spot it could now be found, remembering the pigeons whose graceful aerial movements had once dotted and enchanted Cairo's sky, was there before his eyes. Undeniable, radiant, freely given, a miraculous gift in sight and close at hand.

After an intense practice, the boys had assumed a cross position, floating on their backs like aquatic flowers on water that was now calm, almost reverential. The first glow of dusk had spread across the sky, and the muezzin's call to the first nightly prayer would soon ring out from the minaret of the nearby mosque, a short walk from the pool.

Stay, stay in the water and float, Captain Ni'mat wanted to shout to this adolescence in bloom. Stay in this raw element that suits you so well. Keep away from our shores of defeat, ugliness, and lies. But Captain Ni'mat knew that his silent and desperate entreaty was pointless.

Like him, like his companions, these youths haloed in beauty, these swordfish with slender bodies, these torpedo fish charged with thunder and electricity, would sooner or later tread on dry ground. Grow heavy. Their elastic feline gait would transform into the penguin's comic waddle or the seal's labored drag.

The final piercing, wistful notes of the muezzin's call to the first nightly prayer were fading when Captain Ni'mat finally decided to rise and join his companions preparing to leave the pool. As he walked toward them, he couldn't stop himself from turning around to contemplate once again, with the same amazement, the young swimmers who had exited the water and were running, laughing, to the changing room.

To his companions' dirty jokes, he merely responded with one of those agreed-upon phrases that Arabic, still a sacralized language, brings mechanically to one's lips: "Satan be cursed!"

But in his mind, Captain Ni'mat was asking himself this question, not knowing whether its author was a debauched libertine or a dazzled Sufi: "O Lord, you created beauty for us in the form of a *fitna* and you ordered us to worship only you. You are beautiful and you love beauty; how then could your creatures remain indifferent and not succumb to it?"

In classical Arabic, the word *fitna* means both seduction and disorder, civil war—of the kind that can tear apart a person as easily as a city.

2

REGARDLESS OF THE AUTHOR of that reflection, when the beauty that had revealed itself to Captain Ni'mat in the pool, at dusk, reappeared to him at night, in a dream, it was indisputably the work of Satan. Whom Captain Ni'mat reflexively cursed three times, upon awakening from this dream unable to determine whether it had been a reverie or a nightmare, or a bit of both at the same time.

The afternoon's young swimmers, easily slicing through the water once practice was over, to then float on its surface like aquatic roses or pond lilies, had appeared to him again in his sleep, but they had undergone a troubling metamorphosis.

Swim trunks clinging to their buttocks, as were the caps on their heads, giving them an ovoid shape, both articles the same bright blue as the horn-rimmed goggles with foggy lenses that masked their eyes, the swimmers resembled celestial creatures fallen from an unknown heaven. But were they merciful creatures or exterminating angels? They all looked alike, seeming clones of the same teenage boy. A teenage boy with a particular androgynous beauty, cold and chilling.

Despite their fogged-up goggles, their collective gaze was clearly aimed at Captain Ni'mat, the only bather at the pool, beneath the pergola where he had taken refuge. The sinister caw of a crow slowly whirling above his head intensified the feeling of impotent solitude and oppressive anxiety gripping him. Abruptly, the clones with ovoid heads and impassive faces extended their right arms in one synchronized movement, pointing at him with accusatory index fingers. In the same instant, the sinister crow, after a last spin carried out at dizzying speed and a final, deafening caw, soared into the air and disappeared. But the strangeness persisted, beating its wings silently above the pergola, above the pool. In terror, Captain Ni'mat realized that his feet were refusing to obey him. He was frozen like a statue.

Suddenly, he sensed something faint, almost imperceptible, a tremor of light perhaps, or a quiver in the air, he didn't really know what it was, but he was sure that this thing was already chipping away at the horrific citadel of strangeness in which he, rendered powerless, was walled.

His premonition was founded, for he soon saw the imperceptible, mysterious thing begin to take form. A faint rustling was coming from the water, which was being lapped by waves so tiny at their birth that they were mere hints. But with dizzying swiftness these waves acquired such amplitude and intensity that they provoked, in the very center of the pool, the most beautiful and improbable of geysers, propelling it to the sky with a single thrust, in a spurting, irrepressible vertical motion. Within that unrestrained, rumbling liquid column, Captain Ni'mat glimpsed what he first took for a strange and magnificent fish before realizing that it was a human figure that, once it descended, began to vigorously cut through the water in his direction. When it emerged from the pool, he was astounded to see a sumptuous body rise before him, dripping in its radiant nudity. It was Islam, his young Nubian houseboy!

Without a word or glance at his master, Islam set one knee on the ground and took the position of an archer bending his bow and ready to loosen his arrows, though he was in reality carrying no such weapon. Nonetheless, this simple but combative posture brought about the disappearance, as if by magic, of the legion of androgynous and menacing clones. It was only then

that this miraculous archer, emerging from some unknown aquatic depths, stood and, turning his face toward his master, gave him a beaming smile.

In his nightmare that had transformed into a strange,
though wonderful, dream, Captain Ni'mat wondered
how he could have remained blind to beauty that had
been before his very eyes every day, for nearly one
year now. In his dream, he wondered whether he was
dreaming, for the archer who had miraculously sur-
faced from the waves in the form of his houseboy was
walking back to the edge of the pool, visibly intent on
returning to the unknown Atlantis from which he had
emerged. Panicked by the thought that the clones would
return as soon as his young savior dove into the water,
Captain Ni'mat, no longer paralyzed, ran toward him.
Involuntarily, as if the boy's radiant nudity, soon to
blend again with that of the water, was so powerfully
suggestive that it dictated his motions, he slid the form-
less swim trunks he was wearing down his legs. When
the naked captain dove after the naked body drawing
him like a magnet, he was shocked by the world he discovered. Where was the familiar pool water, clear as
crystal on certain days and less so on others, always
slightly tinged with chlorine, contained but continu-
ally refreshed by an ingenious system that welcomed
bodies and amenably cooled them off? Where was that

miraculous and mystery-free water? Captain Ni'mat had dived into the familiar water of a familiar pool, but the waters which now surrounded his body were dense, murky, and frozen in oppressive silence.

And in these waters, the sumptuous body that had risen into the sky, encased in a liquid, sonorous geyser, a radiantly naked body that had taken the position of an archer-savior a few moments prior, was no more than a fishlike shadow that was growing distant, sinking deeper and deeper. Close to suffocation, Captain Ni'mat, who had vainly tried to catch that shadow, returned to the surface where he noted, in alarm, that the pool was now surrounded on all sides by the same threatening azure beings. "What did I do to you?" he shouted, sitting up abruptly and violently in his bed, body dripping with sweat. His wife was sleeping soundly, or perhaps had only been partially awakened by his shout, as she rolled over and continued her momentarily interrupted snoring. For some time, Captain Ni'mat had been thinking that they should get separate bedrooms, because of that snoring, which was worsening with age.

Heart still racing, he left the bed and went into the bathroom to splash some water on his face, but changing his mind, he headed straight into the shower. After bathing at this unusual hour, and then drying off, he threw on a sleeveless jalabiya made of thin, light fabric and went out into the garden, hoping for one of those gentle breezes that were like a heaven-sent gift in this city and this country penned in by desert.

His hope was dashed. Not the slightest wind, not the slightest quiver of a breeze, rustled the leaves of trees cast in a silvery, spectral glow by the moonlight. The trunks looming tall and still, silent and stubborn, provoked a strange unease in him, as though they were sentinels watching him, reproaching him for this odd, nocturnal stroll. What's the meaning of this dream that seems to be following me? wondered Captain Ni'mat, still ill at ease. The image of his houseboy as he had appeared in his dream opportunely came to the captain's rescue, redirecting his confused and troubled thoughts toward the village where Islam was from: Kom Ombo. The boy's parents had told him how the government settled them in this village near Aswan after the region in which they had been living, Nubia, was swallowed up by the waters of Lake Nasser, following the erection of the High Dam. It was as if Islam, who was born in Kom Ombo and had never seen the land of his ancestors, submerged Nubia, had nonetheless begun his swim from that new Atlantis to then emerge from the geyser in the captain's dream and, taking the position of the nude archer, rid him of his clone tormentors.

Content with this poetic explanation, Captain Ni'mat was even more pleased when he found another explanation, which struck him as brilliant, for the combative posture adopted by Islam. In one of the many temples found throughout Upper Egypt, he had seen, engraved in stone, a fresco depicting the pharaoh's army, which included Nubian archers, one knee on the ground and drawn bow in hand. Surprised, he realized that his strange dream was nonetheless internally coherent and drew from authenticated historical events, both contemporary and those dating back over two thousand years. To say nothing of the core of this dream, which concerned him personally, the most intimate part of him, and which had something to do with—he felt this so strongly—beauty. Beauty as a belated revelation, as simultaneous promise and threat, consoling and troubling beauty, one and many, shimmering, mysterious, ambiguous, undecidable.

First, those youthful androgynous swimmers appearing to him in two wildly antithetical forms: diurnal, as magnificent creatures resembling both fish and flower; and nocturnal, as azure beings, clones of one chilling, beautiful figure. Next, the long-ignored and ultimately lifesaving beauty in clear sight, in the guise of his houseboy Islam transfigured in a dream into a miraculous archer.

Captain Ni'mat could feel his heart pounding wildly. He wasn't dreaming, he was face-to-face with reality, and this tangible reality was even more splendid, even more sublime than what he had seen in the dream. Without realizing it, immersed in his thoughts, Captain Ni'mat had reached the hut in which Islam slept, located in the back of the garden. The door wasn't closed, and thanks to the moonlight he could see the radiant nudity that had dazzled him in his dream and attracted him like a magnet.

Islam was sleeping on his back. His supple, ivory-bright body, though the skin was certainly quite soft, seemed to radiate the sharpness, rigidity, and hardness of ebony. But in the night silence, as if to counterbalance these almost quantifiable physical traits, to soften this geometry of clean, harsh lines, a pistil of splendid beauty had bloomed between the sleeper's thighs, as if inside the corolla of a flower, and was quivering, it too in silence. A soft, trembling, and carnal pistil, its supple flesh ample and nonetheless—Captain Ni'mat understood, or rather intuited, this overwhelming revelation—the very center of that clean, harsh geometrical grid: the radiant source and incandescent hearth of the radioactivity soundlessly emitted by the sleeping adolescent's body.

Before gently closing the door on this sleeper who was now revealing himself to be just as threatening, though a different kind of threat, as the azure beings who had appeared in his still recent dream, Captain Ni'mat stood frozen in place for a long moment, both fascinated and horrified.

As he slowly returned to the villa, he was no longer wondering whether the beauty that had brought upon his stunned state was a divine epiphany or a satanic temptation, but quite simply what upsets this belated yet blistering revelation would introduce into his life.

3

Darling,

*I heard you get up in the middle of the night and
I didn't want to wake you. I'm off to the club. Your
mangua juice is in the fridge.*

Your Mervet

Captain Ni'mat, suffering from insomnia, had only
fallen back asleep once dawn neared. When he awoke,
he found his wife's thoughtful note on his bedside
table and felt grateful for her and it. For years, she had
faithfully prepared him a delicious juice every morning, with *mangua* as today, but also with other fruits,
gawafra, fraisa, lamoun, bourtouqal, mouz, touffah, 'inab,
depending on the season and whatever happened to
inspire her.

The daughter of a major landowner, Mervet had nonetheless chosen to marry for love, though Ni'mat had not yet attained the rank of captain, but was merely a noncommissioned officer pilot fresh out of the Air Academy. From the very start of their relationship, she had called him "my falcon," or "my Horus," which was the name of the god with the head of that predatory bird. Although Ni'mat came from a modest family of teachers, Mervet's father didn't see his daughter's marriage as an unsuitable match. On the contrary, by allying himself with an officer with vocal socialist leanings, this high-ranking member of the Wafd, a political party that found itself, like all the rest, on the wrong side of the law, had avoided the extreme measures of the new regime. Though a good share of his lands fell subject to expropriation laws, he was not brought to court like countless other important party figures.

Only a few days after their engagement ceremony (but this was planned), Ni'mat had left for Russia, for a yearlong training program in Moscow. Upon his return, three months after their wedding celebration, when Mervet was pregnant with their first child, his first baptism by fire would be in Yemen. Egypt had sent an expeditionary force there to support the young republic, which was battling the Imam's followers and their Saudi military backers. All this to say that the first years of Ni'mat and Mervet's marriage were hardly idyllic. All the more so as their political ideas were in total opposition. However, the young air force officer's influence over his wife was so considerable, and Mervet's love for her falcon so strong, that not only did she come to view the intervention in Yemen as legitimate, she even became a fervent supporter of the Arab brand of socialism espoused by the new regime.

Drinking the cool, delicious mango juice, Captain Ni'mat gloomily thought back to those years, when they had been so young and enthusiastic, when their dreams, like their love, had been so vast.

Dreams that they had each betrayed, in their own way, and sometimes together. Four years before his engagement, Ni'mat had made a decision that forced his life into a radical junction. That ill-fated decision was his first betrayal, though he couldn't have known it then. But now, he was certain that by prioritizing patriotic duty over his passion, literature, he had betrayed the purest, strongest, most authentic, and most mysterious part of himself. The captain still remembered, though the exact phrasing eluded him, Kafka's reflections about literature, which had greatly impacted the humanities student he had been at the beginning of his university studies. Literature as a leap beyond the killers' ranks, literature as the ax to crack the frozen sea within us—that, in essence, was the grandiose and lifesaving mission the ascetic from Prague ascribed to literature. Except that Ni'mat had forgotten Kafka's lesson and found himself in the killers' ranks, spinning his death machine over the sky of Arabia Felix, as Yemen was once called, spitting out fire like a monstrous dragon onto peaceful oases where life would then blaze, burn, retract, and shrivel, carbonizing and cooling bit by bit, slowly, inexorably, until it was reduced to a frozen husk.

Dreams betrayed! Mervet had enlisted the services of a lawyer to prove that she met the conditions stipulated by the recent government decree, which allowed former landowners expropriated under the Nasser regime, or their beneficiaries, to reacquire their land. Captain Ni'mat, the former Nasserian and Marxist sympathizer, was no less motivated than his wife in this endeavor. Nowadays, he felt genuine sympathy for the dispossessed former landowners, some of whom had struggled too, slogging away before acquiring their wealth, unlike the nouveaux riches whom he despised. What would our lives have been like, he wondered, if there hadn't been the Free Officers' coup d'état? Though in that case, would Mervet's father have agreed to marry off his daughter (what's more his only daughter) to an officer who, yes, was serving in the most prestigious branch of the military but whose pay was piddling compared to the fortune she would one day inherit?

After drinking his mango juice, Captain Ni'mat didn't put on his tracksuit for his daily jog, which he usually took early, before the alleys and boulevards of the Ma'adi neighborhood succumbed to car pollution and a scorching sky. Instead he took a shower, threw on his thin summer jalabiya, and summoned Islam for his massage. The young servant's duties included, in addition to housework, groceries, walking the dog, and watering and maintaining the garden, the regenerative massage he gave the captain after his jog and morning shower.

The young Nubian had learned the art of massage with disconcerting rapidity. For a time, Captain Ni'mat had brought him to the club so that the masseur Abu Hassan, who worked in a tiny room adjoining the showers and the sauna, could teach him the basic techniques of his art. However, the student quickly surpassed the master, and Captain Ni'mat soon came to prefer Islam's hands, which were long and delicate, to Abu Hassan's powerful, expert ones.

The waves of sensual pleasure felt by Captain Ni'mat during the massage sessions had always struck him as completely natural and in no way suspect. In Arab-Islamic civilization, the public bath (the hammam) is an emblematic institution where the art of massage has been practiced for centuries. That long history peeks through in the very origin of the word "massage," which comes from the Arab term *mass*, meaning "to touch, palpate."

But today, when Captain Ni'mat summoned Islam, an entire erotic culture associated with the hammam abruptly came to his mind, namely a few licentious stories that crudely related what some regulars of public baths went there looking for in the first place. He himself recognized that the sensations he experienced beneath Islam's oil-covered fingers were of a far different nature than those prompted by Abu Hassan's thick hands and his pudgy, though still soft, fingers. What was the club masseur hiding behind his calm manner, thoughtful air, and dignified, serious face? Before now, Captain Ni'mat hadn't wanted to give the slightest credence to the rumors circulating about certain club members who hurried, almost on a daily basis, into the tiny room adjoining the sauna, where Abu Hassan had presided for over two decades.

Islam didn't come right away, and Ni'mat, annoyed, went into the garden and called him again. The house-boy, who was trimming a rosebush and hadn't heard his master's first summons, ran toward him, the smile on his lips natural but with an obsequious, servile undertone created by fear. He was sweaty, suffocating—especially in this heat—in a shapeless gray jalabiya of questionable cleanness. But the captain, after his dream and nocturnal garden stroll, now knew what blazing beauty, and what promises and threats, were hiding beneath those rags. He made a harsh face and reprimanded his servant: "You animal, how many times have I told you to wash and change your clothes more often? Go take a shower, then come give me a massage."

"*Hader*, Captain."

Hader—"present"—is how the majority of Egyptians answer when they're asked something. Islam had automatically responded with this word expressing acquiescence, though he remembered that the shower reserved for servants, at the back of the garden, was out of order. When he informed his master, the captain again called him an animal and asked why he hadn't told him earlier.

"I informed hanem Mervet, Captain."

Captain Ni'mat was reminded that when Islam had any request to make, be it personal or related to his many tasks, the boy always addressed his wife. Do I terrorize him that much, he wondered, or is it simply the natural manifestation of a collective, ancient fear inspired by those who possess the slightest ounce of power or wealth in this country in those who lack it? In a softer voice, he said to his young frightened servant, "Well, you'll just have to clean yourself in the villa shower."

Islam's eyes, which were slightly slanted, became round like two marbles. Captain Ni'mat had expected his suggestion to astonish his servant, and he told him, smiling, "I know, the hanem won't be happy, but we don't have to tell her. So, go get some clean clothes now, something light, to put on after your shower instead of that awful jalabiya."

Captain Ni'mat was fully aware that he was engaging in a sort of transgression by suggesting that his servant enter one of his masters' most intimate spaces, and by establishing a complicity with the boy behind his wife's back. But that complicity struck him as indispensable, for today—he felt this so keenly—he was seeking something more than physical relaxation from the massage he would receive from Islam, who had gone to wash up. The captain had decided, in order to gain some interior clarity, to abandon himself completely and without resistance to the disquiet he had experienced the first time the young Nubian's fingers quivered across his skin like tiny grass snakes. A sensation that he had also occasionally felt beneath the club masseur's pudgy fingers, though he had never let those waves of disconcerting pleasure spread through his body and interfere at will. As soon as he sensed them coming, he always found an excuse to say something, some phrase that would deflect, like a thunderbolt off a lightning rod, a sensual pleasure both desired and feared.

For example: "Oh, that's more of a pinch, Abu Hassan!"

To which the stern masseur would respond with a technical explanation: "Actually that is what we call a pinch. You see, captain, there are parts of the body that need to be pinched, others barely grazed, and some, on the contrary, kneaded at length."

"Ah! Well, then ignore me, you know what to do better than I."

During this brief exchange, the troubling sensation would be expelled, and the club masseur would fall silent once more, his expert fingers alone conversing with a body whose slightest reactions they could detect. In the course of these sessions, Captain Ni'mat had learned the names of the various massage techniques.

There was, in addition to pinching, *effleurage* (grazing), *petrissage* (kneading), pummeling, hacking, percussion, pressure, *tapotement*, vibration, and surely Abu Hassan had only taught him part of a lexicon that must be far richer.

These suggestive technical terms only heightened the impatience and apprehension—akin to that of waiting for a lover—felt by Captain Ni'mat, who found that his young masseur was taking his time with the unprecedented shower he had suggested. The captain eventually approached the bathroom, whose door opened as he was preparing to call his servant. Islam had put on a white T-shirt and a black pair of shorts, and on his feet, light sandals. Warm and translucent drops of water were still dripping down his face. His slightly plump lips parted, and this separation lit up his face. A typically Nubian beauty! thought Captain Ni'mat as he grabbed a bottle of eau de toilette and told Islam, "Hold out your hands." And when the boy rubbed his face: "Look at you all nice and clean! Plus you're much better off in those light clothes than in that awful shapeless sack of a jalabiya you were floating around in. I'm going to give you one hundred pounds so you can buy yourself another T-shirt and another pair of shorts."

Islam thanked his master and went into his hut to drop off the clothes he had been wearing before the shower. Captain Ni'mat, clad only in his underwear, stretched out on his stomach on a mattress, and when Islam returned, he told him, simultaneously feeling his heart beat faster: "Get on the mattress behind me. You'll be more comfortable."

Islam, mildly surprised, complied but only on the farthest edge of the mattress, which was almost entirely occupied by the captain's body. The captain leaned around and asked Islam to stand, after which he spread his legs and said: "Get on your knees, between my legs. It'll be easier for you."

Increasingly troubled by this new behavior, which he found very odd, Islam did as he was asked and realized that his master was in fact right. Kneeling in line with the axis of the captain's body, he could massage it from ankles to neck, in one sweeping, continuous, and fluid movement. Captain Ni'mat also felt the change, and this time he was determined not to use a verbal lightning rod to deflect and curb the sensations that might disconcert him. But as soon as he sensed that the first ripple of that invisible tide was about to emerge, he recalled one of the terms from Abu Hassan's technical lexicon, twisted around toward the young Nubian boy kneeling behind him, and said: "You know, the movement you just did is called the *petrissage*. That's French for kneading."

Islam felt like laughing but he held back. The image of his mother kneading bread dough, far away in their village of Kom Ombo, had suddenly crossed his mind, and he was torn between nostalgia and laughter.

Captain Ni'mat was annoyed at himself for talking and tried to empty his mind, to relax his body so fully that he was nothing but skin, his tactile sense on alert. With his eyes and his fingertips, Islam noted this relaxation, an abandonment that was almost a bodily offering made him by his master. It was then that his fingers, instinctually, began a wordless dialogue with the thickset body he felt gradually loosening and softening in their wake.

Captain Ni'mat reveled in this silent dialogue. The instant he wanted the pressure to become a little firmer, he felt the young Nubian's palms magically press even harder. It was a conversation held skin to skin, in an extraordinary tactile language that Captain Ni'mat, stupefied, delighted, and wondering if it was the same for the young Nubian, was discovering, learning how to spell its first letters. The technical terms Abu Hassan had taught him seemed so dry and limited now, compared to the richness, polysemy, and infinite nuances of this new magical language! This delicate quiver sprouting in the tender, tiny hollows at the tops of his thighs that was spreading trembling waves across his buttocks! Completely naturally, without the slightest embarrassment, Captain Ni'mat raised his butt slightly, baring it halfway by partially lowering his briefs, and ordered the young Nubian, "Massage me here," adding, as if to justify himself, "the blood needs to circulate through the whole body."

Islam, hesitant, barely grazed the captain's buttocks, his hands instead lingering closer to the tender hollows precisely where the delicate quiver spreading waves of subtle pleasure had originated. Captain Ni'mat, annoyed, lowered his briefs completely, with a single movement, and insisted in a commanding voice: "I told you, the buttocks! And not those light strokes, knead them with some muscle in it!"

This time, again thinking about his mother kneading dough, Islam couldn't keep from laughing. Captain Ni'mat didn't reprimand or insult him as he feared, but on the contrary encouraged him. "Good, that's exactly it, but with even more muscle."

Islam, the reluctant and impromptu baker, put all his energy into kneading and working this dough of flesh, on both sides, while thinking that in his village, any man who dared request such a service would be immediately called a *khawala* and spat upon. Here, in Cairo, conventions were very different, and perhaps Captain Ni'mat's demand was quite natural, even though during the club massage sessions he had observed, Islam didn't remember ever seeing the buttocks exposed. Perhaps this unprecedented, immodest stripping down could be explained by the fact that with Islam, younger than Abu Hassan and a mere servant, Captain Ni'mat felt no embarrassment and was free to express his most intimate desires without shame. After all, now he was pulling up his briefs with utter nonchalance, and complimenting the young Nubian: "You were perfect, Islam. That will be all for today."

Then he rose, gave the boy a gentle pat on the shoulder, and said, "Here, I'm going to give you the hundred pounds I promised you so you can buy some light summer clothes." When he placed the money in Islam's hands, he added, with a smile: "As for the shower you took here, don't worry about it. The hanem won't know a thing."

Islam thanked him profusely and was about to return to the garden but Captain Ni'mat held him back and laughingly said, "And don't go telling your little friends in the neighborhood that Captain Ni'mat asked you to massage his ass."

Islam simply placed his joined index and middle fingers over his lips, as though he was sewing his mouth shut with a needle and thread. Captain Ni'mat, after patting his shoulder again, gave him a firm, friendly handshake.

Equal to equal, partners in crime.

4

MERVET HAD JOINED her friends at the club pool,
which was reserved for women on Saturdays and Mon-
days, from ten a.m. to two p.m., because of the *muhajja-*
bat for whom it was out of the question to reveal their
swimsuit-clad bodies to the lustful male gaze.

Mervet didn't wear the veil but because her two
closest friends, Chaïma and Faïha, did, having be-
grudgingly resigned themselves under pressure from
their husbands and their daughters who, though they
had only just reached puberty, were already veiled
themselves, she went to the pool on the two days reserved for women. There, the three friends, all well into
their fifties, also found themselves, like their husbands,
in the same niggling, mismatched confrontation. Starting at noon, the members of the girls' youth swim team
would invade their peaceful world and force them to

return to shore where, after briefly exposing themselves to the sun—unlike European women with their
irrepressible desire for a tan, Mervet and her friends
were intent on maintaining the whiteness of their
skin—they would sit at the table reserved for their husbands beneath the pergola.

At the sight of the young swimmers in the prime
of youth, the women sank into melancholy daydreams.
They were almost ashamed to inquire about each other's
health, to mention their minor aches or more serious is-
sues, like diabetes or rheumatism, to compare the various
diets they'd adopted to lose weight, without effect. They
preferred to talk about their younger days, when they
had been as graceful, supple, and free as these young
girls frolicking in the water as they looked on admir-
ingly. Though they wondered whether that joie de vivre,
that freedom, was merely a brief interlude in these young
girls' lives, given the oppressive fundamentalist climate
now permeating all of Egyptian society.

"Mervet, your two daughters are lucky to be studying abroad. When I see mine…barely nubile and
talking to me like theologians from Al Azhar!"

Mervet pointed out that perhaps Chaïma and her
husband bore some responsibility for this change in
their daughters. "Why," she asked, "did you give in to
Behjat and your girls, and start wearing the veil?"

"Quite simply, my dear Mervet, for some peace."

"A slave's peace," replied Mervet bluntly, instantly regretting her harshness and affectionately squeezing her friend's hands.

Chaïma took no offense and tried to justify herself: "Your husband Ni'mat has always had more progressive ideas about the female condition. He even had some Marxist notions at one point."

"A lot of good it did him! And anyway, that's all ancient history. He's done deluding himself."

Faïha, silent until then, asked Mervet, "Where are you in the process of getting your family's land back?"

"My lawyer tells me that we're on the right track, but he keeps asking me for more money, supposedly to grease the bureaucratic wheels. Maybe he's being honest, but I don't trust the greedy little shark. They're all the same."

Chaïma abruptly changed the subject to one that was certain to be more cheerful and lighthearted, judging from the giggly enthusiasm with which she announced: "Look who just got here—Froggy! Our vanquishing swimmers better watch out..."

The woman with whom they had stuck that nickname came to the pool every day, at the same time. It was impossible not to notice her arrival. Eyes hidden by black sunglasses, mouth painted with outrageous lipstick, she would head to the changing room, perched on stiletto heels and head carried high, without a hello or wave to anyone, followed by two female servants, the first with a crammed bag over her shoulder, and the second, a smaller bag in her hand. The first would hurry into the changing room after her mistress to help her into a swimming garment that more closely resembled a diving suit. The second would fetch a chair that she placed near one of the two corners of the pool with a metal ladder, and, opening her small bag, pull out fins that she would shortly put on her mistress's feet, seated on the chair placed there for precisely that reason. Also from her bag came a bottle of white cream that she would rub over her mistress's face just before she entered the water and, for when she came back out, a small towel to dry her face and a sort of cape of thin fabric which she would place over her mistress's back, in order to forestall a sudden chill.

During this time, in the changing room, the first servant would help her mistress pull on a thick black leather wetsuit that clung to her entire body, neck to ankle. Once she put on black plastic goggles, protection for her eyes irritated no doubt by the chlorine-enhanced pool water, and a cap in the same black shade as everything else, the frog woman would disappear into this night from which nothing emerged except a plump mouth reddened by scarlet lipstick. Then, like a priestess performing an ancient and mysterious lustral ritual of purification and regeneration, the strange woman would slowly make her way toward the metal ladder, whose few rungs she cautiously began to descend after the second servant had first placed the fins on her feet. When the water reached her chest, her hands would release the two sides of the ladder and she would commence, near the edge of the pool, lengthwise laps that lasted exactly one hour. A slow, sweeping breaststroke, without pause. None of the young girls dared cross the intangible, invisible frontier that demarcated the aquatic corridor tacitly and imperatively reserved by the woman as soon as she entered the water. Her silent and calm strokes, made in slow and even rhythm, exuded strength and determination, something stubborn, cruel, and implacable that inspired their respect. The young swimmers in the adjoining lane would be fascinated by this gigantic black frog whose mouth opened and closed at regular intervals, like a carnivorous, bloody flower.

"She looks like a leech!"

"A vampire!"

"God forgive us for badmouthing this woman, who might be suffering from some kind of terrible skin disease, to cover up like that."

"Maybe she's just a little nuts."

"Even if that's the case, and however unpleasant and standoffish she may be, you have to admit she's braver than us. She doesn't let those girls take over the whole pool."

"Actually, ladies, how come we're just sitting around under this pergola? Why don't we dive in too and show some solidarity with our valiant and solitary water Amazon?"

The suggestion came from Mervet, who immediately put it into action, rising swiftly and heading, like a wrestler entering the ring, to the pool right beside them. Her two friends, faster, passed her and dove in at the same time. But she was quick to join them and it was she, with her imposing body and sweeping breaststroke, who carved them a path through the young wriggling bodies. Soon, with a joyful competitive spirit that revived the vivacity and vigor of their youth, the three friends were each able to conquer their own lane, like their wild sister who had set the example. The four adult women now occupied nearly half of the pool, lengthwise. But though the three friends were delighted, and expressed their delight through a variety of swimming moves, the solitary woman changed nothing of the form and rhythm of her regular and unrelenting breaststroke. Mervet, who was closest to her, proffered a sincere smile meant as an invitation for an introduction. The sole response was a mouth that opened wide but then closed immediately after, without hesitation, in the way of a carnivorous flower snatching its prey. Mervet saw her two friends smirking at her disappointment and sprayed jets of water in their faces, before joining them to sum up the situation: "May as well talk to a frog, indeed!"

The three friends continued to swim a while longer, maintaining a constant stream of jokes. Deep down, they were grateful to this strange, unapproachable woman, who had enabled them to swim as they hadn't in quite some time. When they emerged from the water and stretched out on a cluster of loungers, they looked at each other smiling. They felt as if they had achieved a victory—they had become young again—the duration of a carefree, liberating swim. But when the frog woman emerged from the water, on the surface of which the young swimmers, practice now over, were floating and drifting like lily pads, the three friends were brought back to harsh reality.

They each closed their eyes and sank into melancholy daydreams.

5

BEFORE THE UNPRECEDENTED MASSAGE he gave his
master, Islam had taken Bobby out early for his daily
morning walk. Bobby was the name Mervet had chosen for a small puppy she'd brought back from England,
and which was now a mountain of flesh ready to leap at
the first stranger he saw. The short-snouted mastiff had
an atavistic belligerence in his eyes, even when playing
as he was now, scampering between Captain Ni'mat,
who was reading his newspaper, and Islam, who had
gone back to trimming the rosebushes. Bobby was
excited by the captain's uncustomary presence at this
hour. Each time the dog approached, Captain Ni'mat
would lift his gaze from the paper and pet him distract-
edly, looking at Islam instead. When the mastiff went
back to the servant, standing on his hind legs, forelegs
around the boy's waist, the contrast created by the two

intertwined bodies was striking. On one side, nervous power and a concentration of muscle that hid a ferocity ready to explode at any moment; on the other, a feline, all grace, with supple hands floating amid the roses like branches. *God, they're young, and so alive!* Captain Ni'mat would think each time he paused his reading to observe them. So far from the pages of ugliness and lies, of scandals, famines, and wars to which he would then return, increasingly distracted. When Islam had completed his task and informed his master that he was leaving to do the food shopping, the captain told him to take Bobby. Islam had no desire to do so, as once again he'd be obliged to restrain him from jumping on the first passerby who walked too close to them. He wrapped the leash around the dog's neck and, threatening him with his index finger, harshly told him, "You better behave, Bobby, or else—!"

The dog's only response was to bare his gleaming canines and begin pulling on the leash.

Once he was a few narrow streets away from the villa, Islam ran into Samir, a Nubian like him, whom everyone called Uncle Samir and who was the walking memory of this neighborhood where he had been working and living for over two decades. Nothing happened without his knowledge, thanks to the vast network of his compatriots employed here. Though, Nubian or not, all those employed by the neighborhood's wealthy residents—guards, chauffeurs, cooks, errand boys, gardeners, and many who, like Islam, served all these roles at once while living under their master's roof—confided in Uncle Samir. Through them, he was made aware of the most intimate and most clandestine facets of life inside the opulent villas hidden among greenery and flowers, their facades unfailingly silent. Uncle Samir would centralize the information, like the chief of an intelligence agency, and on countless occasions the police had in fact turned to him, though to no avail. Interested in and informed of everything, Uncle Samir nonetheless intended to take all the secrets he had amassed to his grave. The information circulated in one direction: he received it, stored it, and interpreted it as he saw fit, but shared it with nobody. Curiously enough, his young colleagues accepted this uneven exchange and took pleasure in recounting the latest rumors or tragedies unfolding around them. Uncle Samir's smiling, lustrous face, his attentive way of listening with a gentle nod, and the words of wisdom offered once his informer had gotten whatever it was off his chest made for the most understanding and surest of confidants. With him, there was no risk of any

trouble from divulging the possibly vile acts or miscon-
duct committed by one's master.

Islam was delighted when he spotted Uncle Samir's
regal, slender body, crowned with an impressive and im-
maculate turban. He had a smile on his face as always,
and he addressed his young fellow Nubian with the
same never-changing phrase, "Well, son, what's new?"

The fact that he had already seen Islam walking the
dog that very morning, and that they'd had a good long
chat, didn't mean that nothing had happened since,
that Islam couldn't be the bearer of interesting, brand-
new tidbits.

"Oh, nothing much, Uncle Samir."

Samir, the ever-attentive observer, didn't agree.
"You already walked Bobby this morning," he said,
adding with a laugh, "The dog in heat or something?"

But the second he made the joke, he remembered
that Bobby had been castrated the previous summer,
and berated himself for the lapse in memory.

"I'm getting old, son. I forgot that I saw hanem
Mervet in tears when Captain Ni'mat carried poor,
emasculated Bobby out of the veterinarian's."

"I took him out because he was bothering the captain while he was reading his newspaper. And speaking of, Uncle Samir, this morning the captain acted a
little strangely with me."

Not a gleam of curiosity shone in the eyes of this universal confidant. As though he hadn't heard what Islam had just said, he was attentively watching a veiled woman hurry to her car and speed away once she was behind the wheel.

"That's hanem Zaïnab. She's in a rush because today the club pool is only reserved for women until two p.m. What were you saying, son?"

"The captain... he was acting strange this morning."

"Really? He's normally so composed."

"He let me take a shower inside the villa."

"Is the garden one not working?"

"No."

"Then he must have been bothered by the smell of sweat about you. You should wash yourself and change your clothes more often. That T-shirt and those shorts are better suited to the season and to your age. Leave the jalabiyas to us old men."

"The captain said the same thing. He even gave me a hundred pounds to buy another outfit, just like the one I'm wearing now."

"Well, what's so strange about that? The captain was kind and generous with you, and you ought to be grateful."

"It's just... I'm afraid of saying something stupid, Uncle Samir."

"Go on, son. You know you can tell Uncle Samir anything without being afraid."

"Well, today the captain asked me to massage his buttocks. I've been giving him a daily massage for a year now, and he's never asked me for that. He even explained how I was supposed to do it, to knead them like bread dough."

"Ah! So that's what strikes you as odd," responded Uncle Samir with a burst of laughter.

Islam, believing he was revealing a terrible secret, felt mildly annoyed. Uncle Samir regained his composure, and in a gentle, almost medical tone, told the novice the reason for his master's strange request: "You know, son, men have a gland located beneath the bladder, which becomes very sensitive with age. A doctor explained it to me. He said that the gland is called the prostata, or something like that. If you ask me, that explains why your captain—who's not so young anymore—had that sudden urge."

"But Uncle Samir, back home, you know what they would call a man who asks you to massage his ass."

"Back home! But back home, we're not like these effendis who spend all their time parked in a chair. Plus, with us," he continued, bursting into laughter again, "there's not much to massage. We're all muscle."

Islam, no longer annoyed, gave a hearty laugh, too.

"Thank you, Uncle Samir. I was afraid that the captain was a..."

He stopped, not daring to say the blazing word, but Uncle Samir reassured him.

"I know what you're thinking, son, but it's different here than it is back home. People aren't so prudish and a captain, a *liwa*, or even a minister doesn't think it shameful to get massaged completely naked and from every angle by their servant."

The understanding and wise confidant concluded, a mischievous smile widening across his face: "And you might as well take in the view. Not everybody gets to massage the ass of a captain flat on his stomach."

Pleased with his discussion with such a sensible man, who also had a sense of humor, Islam pointed out, "It's not a very pretty view."

"Eh," concluded Uncle Samir, "you can get used to anything."

But after he left the neighborhood sage, whom nothing surprised, whose tranquil mood and calm mind nothing troubled, Islam would have the chance to hear an entirely different interpretation. When he ran into his best friend Mustapha, who like Islam came from Kom Ombo, he once again recounted Captain Ni'mat's strange behavior.

"Damn! Him too?"

"What do you mean, him too?"

"Do you know what Abdu told me? Well! His master started off by asking him to massage his ass too, and when he realized, after the third session, that Abdu was no longer bothered by touching that fleshy, intimate part of his body, that he found it perfectly normal, do you know what his master asked him to do then?"

The question so clearly had a single possible response that Islam merely made a gesture—four fingers of one hand curled into his palm, forming with his thumb a kind of orifice, a narrow passageway into which the middle finger of the other hand burrowed in and out in a rapid motion—that obviously represented an act of penetration, of sodomy. Which Mustapha confirmed, adding, overcome by disdain: "And you know what? The effendi got such a taste for it that he told Abdu that he could no longer make love to his wife except on the days when he got his *attaᵭlik al hamimi*— intimate massage—which is what the two of them call it now."

Islam thought back to Uncle Samir's comments about how the prostata could become hypersensitive among men of a certain age. But could it make them *khawalat*, he wondered, troubled by what Mustapha had just revealed. His friend cautioned him, "Careful, Islam. Don't tell anyone what I just told you."

Islam, his index and middle fingers joined, again pretended to sew his lips shut as he had when Captain Ni'mat asked for discretion. Was his master, Islam suddenly wondered, his heartbeat accelerating, already anticipating the next step, which would be to ask him for the most intimate of massages, *attaðlik al hamimi*?

The impatient dog visibly didn't appreciate this second stop that was dragging on, and pulled on the leash growling.

"Easy, you," Islam commanded as he shook a menacing index finger, "otherwise you're gonna get an ass massage too, but not one you'll enjoy."

The two young friends burst out laughing and Islam continued the joke in his head, thinking, "Though, who knows if Bobby, who's no young pup, not to mention castrated, might actually like it if I carried out my threat?"

At these comical and mildly sacrilegious thoughts, Islam cursed Satan and parted ways with his friend.

6

WHEN MERVET RETURNED from the club, Captain Ni'mat had already prepared his swim bag to go to the pool in his turn.

"Did you at least eat something?" his wife asked, as attentive and thoughtful as always.

"Yes, the squab stuffed with rice and chicken liver that was left over from yesterday. Such a treat!"

"Did Islam get the groceries?"

"Yes."

"Good. I'm going to make myself a salad and then dash over to Suzanne's. Today's the final fitting for my new dress."

"Tell her not to make the waist too tight, like she did for the last one."

"I know, you already told me. Don't worry, dear, I know I'm too old for it."

"That's not what I was trying to say, Mervet."

"Of course, dear," she answered with a smile, involuntarily casting him a longing glance whose futility she immediately realized.

The game of seduction was long over. For that matter, was there anyone left in this country who felt the desire to please and seduce, who took pride in their appearance? Judging from all the bodies buried beneath gray, shapeless clothing, the men's gazes lowered over their bushy beards, the women's hair imprisoned by veils, one might think that seduction had become an insult to God and an attack against one's fellow man. Yes, their two daughters were lucky to be studying abroad, but Mervet was consumed by worry about their development once they returned home. The sight of Islam all cleaned up, light, summer garments gracefully clinging to his slender body, snapped her out of her melancholy thoughts.

"You look like a real Cairo native now," she commented with a smile. "Did the plumber come fix the shower?"

"No, hanem," he replied, then, anticipating the next question, "I used a basin to clean myself."

"That was smart. I'm going to call that damn plumber giving me the runaround."

Bobby, emerging from the back of the garden, bounded toward his mistress and wrapped his two raised forelegs around her waist. She stroked the dog's snout, affectionately whispering, "Easy now, easy now, baby boy. At least I can always count on you."

She continued to pet his flat muzzle and thick, muscular neck for a while, as his back quivered with pleasure that was completely invisible in the dog's irremediably aggressive face. When she tried to go back inside the villa, he followed, scampering around her feet and nearly tripping her.

"Has he eaten, Islam?"

"Yes, hanem."

"Then take him to his kennel. You're going to take a nice little nap, aren't you, baby boy?"

Islam drew the massive canine toward him by pretending to run away, and after he put Bobby in the kennel, he returned to his hut to lie down and get some rest himself.

In the dimness, he removed his T-shirt and shorts, stretched his arms, and did a few calisthenic movements similar to those he had seen Captain Ni'mat do. Except now he felt far more handsome, far younger, and even far stronger and more virile than the captain who had long terrified him, only to then, this morning, offer him the most intimate part of his body, to be kneaded like dough, with total and almost feminine abandon. Remembering the moment, Islam got a sudden erection. He removed his briefs, lay down on his stomach on the mat that covered the hut floor, and allowed his unbridled imagination to guide the back-and-forth movement of his hand. And what if what he was imagining could come true, and very soon?

Panting, he began whispering to the imaginary body beneath him: "That's nice, huh? You like it, don't you?" until a gushing ejaculation made him shudder from head to toe, leaving him calm and relaxed in its wake, stretched out completely on his stomach and im-mersed in the most pleasant of naps.

7

CAPTAIN NI'MAT ARRIVED at the pool, always fairly empty on afternoons when it had been reserved for women in the morning. Mirroring the fundamentalists obsessed with the idea of ritual purity, many men preferred to abstain from swimming on days when the pool water had been churned up by the bodies of women who were perhaps on their menstrual cycle.

Apart from two men swimming laps, there were only Captain Ni'mat's friends who, standing in a circle in the pool, water at their waists, were absorbed in their endless, joke-filled chattering. Captain Ni'mat waved hello and went into the changing room. It was empty apart from Abu Hassan, who had clearly just taken a shower and was standing in front of the enormous mirror on the wall, brushing his hair. He was wearing only his briefs, and Captain Ni'mat, who had never seen him dressed so sparsely, admired his well-proportioned physique, unable to avoid glancing at those briefs. He thought to himself that such a body wouldn't look so terrible amidst the young swimmers who would take over the pool in a few hours. Every age in life could bring with it a specific kind of physical beauty, if you didn't let yourself go. He knew a yoga instructor who was in his eighties, but who had maintained the flexibility and vivacity of a young man.

The captain, who had no desire to seek refuge in the shade of the bougainvillea once the swimmers arrived, following their movements in the water from the pergola, admiring and melancholy, asked Abu Hassan if he was free around four p.m.

"Yes," the masseur responded. "There's hardly anyone here today."

"Okay, I'll see you then."

Captain Ni'mat left the changing room and, contrary to habit, didn't use one of the pool's metal ladders. He dove in near his companions with a splash, prompting outbursts of fake indignation. Without responding, he swam away in a vigorous crawl that he maintained at the same rhythm for the entire length of the pool, back and forth. When he finally returned to the group, he was puffing like a whale but smiling contentedly.

"You take yourself for a youngster, is that it?"

"You'd be better off doing the same. Soon those youngsters are going to chase you pathetically out of this pool you take for a sauna built for chitchatting."

The captain studied each of his companions, finding that there was something decadent in this band of talkers—the decadence of the patricians of fifth-century Rome, relaxing and gossiping in the thermal baths as the city crumbled, the empire surrounded by barbarians.

"Why," he asked in a serious tone that took his comrades by surprise, "do you keep up this pointless chatting even in the pool, rather than swimming?"

"Listen to this pretentious bastard, giving us lessons because he swam two laps. My dear captain, conversing is an art in old civilizations like ours."

"So is *nukta*, speaking of nonsense," he retorted ironically, leaving them to resume his swim, still a crawl, but even more vigorous, and more enraged.

Yes, *nukta*—funny anecdotes with a keen dash of wit—and *dardasha*—free-ranging conversations about anything and everything—are the only forms of art we have left, he grumbled to himself as his hands thundered against the water's satiny skin. *Nukta, dardasha,* and a vague, widespread violence, lurking like an animal ready to go for our throats at any moment.

After an hour of this rageful swim, Captain Ni'mat was out of steam. He left the water and went to lie down on a lounger, far from the pergola where Egypt's double, immortal victory would once again be celebrated. The captain, however, preferred to enjoy, in solitude, the tiny victory he had just achieved over habit and lassitude. For he had decided to start exercising again, to discipline and master his body until it was fit to face those of the young swimmers who would soon invade the pool, and to move among them without spoiling their harmony, instead of drifting along like floating, amorphous algae. He wanted to regain his warrior's body.

But Captain Ni'mat would soon realize that this body that he had decided to master and rehabilitate had its own life, logic, and reasons, which didn't necessarily coincide with those of the mind and will.

Shortly before the whooping of adolescents rose within the complex, Captain Ni'mat went to the cramped massage room where he found Abu Hassan waiting for him. The masseur took the captain's large bath towel out of his hands and stretched it across a raised bed at the head of which was placed a small stuffed pillow.

Contrary to habit, Captain Ni'mat lay on his back, and Abu Hassan began without comment. He first massaged the captain's scalp, face, and neck, then his shoulders, arms, chest, stomach, and groin. When he reached that last, sensitive zone, Abu Hassan lowered the captain's briefs slightly and his fingers artfully and delicately switched to something closer to a caress than a massage. His two pinky fingers slid into the creases of the captain's thighs, his thumbs twirled over the top of the pubis, while his other fingers, in a back-and-forth movement that brushed against the genitals, massaged the tender hill of flesh. Captain Ni'mat would frequently, at this moment, feel an erection growing, which he would prevent by saying the first thing that came to mind to Abu Hassan. But today, he closed his eyes and allowed his burgeoning erection to follow its course. Abu Hassan, noting this change, intensified the pressure and rhythm of his massage, his fingers gradually descending lower and caressing the captain's genitals with increasing force. Once the erection had undeniably formed, Captain Ni'mat ever silent, his eyes closed, Abu Hassan, also without a word, purposefully moved the captain's briefs out of the way, grabbed hold of his penis, and began to rub it in an increasingly rapid lateral motion against the pubis. Captain Ni'mat still didn't react, letting it happen, and wondering whether this masseur whom he had always considered so dignified and stern would opt to masturbate him in a more conventional way, rather than merely imposing this exciting but frustrating lateral motion on his now fully erect penis.

"Does that feel good, Captain?"

The question yanked Captain Ni'mat from his illusory frozen state. Opening his eyes, he assented with a nod but realized, horribly disappointed, that his manhood had abruptly slumped during this brief exchange.

"Don't worry about it," said Abu Hassan in a calm and poised voice. "I'll bring you back."

As though he was in an operating room! Amused by this tracksuit-clad anesthesiologist's way of talking, he closed his eyes, curious about what the masseur would do but trustful and consenting from the start. Abu Hassan slid his briefs farther down his legs, removed them, and told the captain, who obeyed immediately, to lie on his stomach while keeping his buttocks slightly raised. Sliding his two hands into the now-liberated narrow space, Abu Hassan grabbed the captain's flaccid penis with one hand and began rubbing it laterally and vigorously against the pubis, while his other hand simultaneously and very gently caressed the perineum. This synchronous two-handed operation prompted a sudden erection from the captain who, without any thought at all, spread his legs as wide as possible and raised his butt even higher. His slightly parted buttocks created a furrow into which the hand caressing his perineum immediately rushed. Now, Abu Hassan was outright massaging the anus with one hand, and Ni'mat, overtaken by such an unprecedented, earth-shattering sensation, began to writhe and moan, without the slightest embarrassment. When he felt a finger, the middle one, smoothly slide into his anus, he didn't have time to cry out in surprise. A sudden ejaculation, anticipated by Abu Hassan, who had rapidly withdrawn his two hands, forced the captain to lie back down. He pushed as hard as he could against the bath towel covering the bed, onto which he released a flood of semen; its abundance shocked him when, as if drunk, he finally sat up and saw the large white stain. Abu Hassan, standing beside him, was visibly satisfied with his successful reanimation effort. He gave the captain a complicit, friendly look, which didn't harbor the slightest glimmer of surprise—or worse, contempt for this aged and respectable man whose most intimate parts he had just explored with his fingers. Fingers that, like the rod that allows the diviner to locate the presence of groundwater, unknown until then, had revealed to Captain Ni'mat a desire buried inside him, boiling but compressed, suppressed. For how many years?

"Lie down on your stomach, Captain. I'm going to massage your back now."

Abu Hassan moved to the head of the bed, so close to Captain Ni'mat that the masseur's penis was almost touching his face. He began to massage the captain's back with a sweeping, regular motion from the neck to the buttocks, which then rose imperceptibly. At one point, Captain Ni'mat's hands, as if guided by a will other than his own, alighted on the masseur's thighs. Abu Hassan nimbly unzipped his fly, took out his penis, and resumed his massage, this time solely of the buttocks. Captain Ni'mat, head lifted, was holding in his hands a restive, formidable penis, which was almost striking him in the face.

The scene—one man having his buttocks massaged as he held the other man's penis—was about to reach its natural conclusion when Captain Ni'mat abruptly thought of the plague of the century. He regretfully released the masseur's penis from his loving grip, rose from the bed, put his swim trunks back on, and said to Abu Hassan: "Let's save that for next time. I'll bring some condoms."

"Yes, Captain. That's more prudent."

"Tell me, Abu Hassan. Aren't you a little surprised by what just happened between us?"

"You know, Captain, I've been doing this job for so many years that nothing surprises me anymore."

"You mean to say..."

"I don't mean to say anything, Captain. Nothing of what happens in this room, which as you can see is sealed like a tomb, travels beyond it."

The analogy wasn't the most joyful, but Captain Ni'mat understood what Abu Hassan meant—that he wouldn't divulge anyone's secrets.

"What I do know, however, Captain, is that the flesh is quite weak and that no one should be judged. No one!"

Captain Ni'mat set a friendly hand on his shoulder and asked him, "How old are you, Abu Hassan?"

"I'm getting on. I just turned fifty."

Captain Ni'mat, embarrassed for the first time to give his age, responded: "Well, what am I supposed to say then? I just passed sixty."

"May God grant you long life, Captain."

"Thank you, Abu Hassan. I have to be off now. Next time I'll bring what's needed."

"Yes, that's best. Now that you've decided to satisfy a desire that many people your age feel but suppress out of shame, you'll feel better."

"How do you know that, Abu Hassan?"

"A doctor explained it to me. Apparently it has to do with the prostata, which becomes very sensitive."

"So that's the reason? It's purely physiological?"

"In any case that was this doctor's opinion."

"A doctor over sixty like me, and who knows this place?" asked Captain Ni'mat slyly.

"Not this 'place,' this 'tomb.' Remember that, Captain," replied Abu Hassan as a broad smile stretched across his stern face.

Captain Ni'mat smiled in turn and took a fifty-pound bill out of the side pocket of his bag: twice the normal cost of the session. But Abu Hassan vigorously refused the bill being handed to him, explaining to the captain: "I don't do this for the money, but for the pleasure I can give respectable people like yourself, who trust me and allow their bodies to freely express themselves in my hands." Then Abu Hassan gave another, mischievously refined smile, and added, "But don't think that it's pity or philanthropy on my part."

"Well then! That's fine, Abu Hassan, but still, this once, accept the fifty-pounder. I'm not offering out of generosity but because I don't have any change."

As he passed Abu Hassan the money, Captain Ni'mat gave him a firm handshake. He left the cramped room described by the man who presided there as a tomb. But to Captain Ni'mat, who had just gotten a taste of forbidden fruit, it seemed like a garden far more enchanted, in far greater bloom, than the familiar pergola toward which he was now heading without any pleasure.

"What's wrong with you? You're walking all wobbly..."

It was with this observation that *liwa* Midhat welcomed him. But it was *liwa* Behjat who responded in lieu of the captain to their perceptive friend: "It's only natural when you take yourself for a youngster and swim like a maniac for over an hour."

Liwa Rif'at proffered another hypothesis: "Unless it's because of an overly energetic massage, as Abu Hassan sometimes inflicts, kneading your body like it's bread dough."

Captain Ni'mat gave *liwa* Rif'at a searching look, wondering if his friend was making a snide insinuation. But he assumed that the reference to kneading dough had just been to make the others laugh, and begin the process that would lead to the creation of a new *nukta*. His theory was confirmed when he heard *liwa* Behjat expand on the image, comparing the body being energetically kneaded by Abu Hassan to beignet dough. From which followed various conjectures about the jobs performed by the grim-faced Abu Hassan before he became a masseur. The *dardasha* and *nukta* motors were all gassed up, and would now run at full throttle.

Captain Ni'mat moved away from the buzzing hive and lay down on a lounger. His gaze lingered on the bodies of a few young swimmers already floating in the water like lily pads. The muezzin's wistful call to the evening's first prayer would soon ring out from the minaret of the nearby mosque.

Captain Ni'mat closed his eyes and thought about his agreement with Abu Hassan, whose stern face was quickly replaced by another. Young, smiling, and with clearly distinguished Nubian features.

II

The Nubian Offering

Serve us your poison, sir, to treat us well!

Minds burning, we know what we have to do,

And plunge to depths of Heaven or of Hell,

To fathom the Unknown, and find the new!

BAUDELAIRE, "VOYAGING"

1

IT HAD BEEN nearly one year since Captain Ni'mat, one sweltering, unforgettable August afternoon, had had the gratifying opportunity to discover another side to the stern masseur who performed his art at the Ma'adi club. More than a discovery, and better, this had been an initiation, and although Abu Hassan had presided, it was Islam who, despite his young age, would nonetheless serve as mystagogue, continue the rites, and introduce the initiate—Captain Ni'mat—to all the secrets and enchantments to which it led.

Islam hadn't been particularly surprised, a few days after his discussion with Uncle Samir and the confidences shared by his friend Mustapha, to observe Captain Ni'mat lying down on his stomach, stark naked, for his daily massage session. And again without much surprise, he watched him spread his legs, raise his butt slightly, and order Islam to massage both his buttocks and his perineum. As soon as the boy complied, Captain Ni'mat's behind began to tremble and at a certain point, sitting up, he showed Islam a condom and bluntly said, "You're going to take off your shorts and roll this onto your penis."

Islam, who had never seen a condom before, looked in astonishment at the little rubber hood: completely limp, translucent, and lightly oiled. He asked what it was.

"Take off your shorts. I'm going to put it on you, but you need to be hard first."

This wasn't difficult for Islam, whose penis, mere seconds after his soft hand began to stroke it, was raising, as a stake would a tent, the shorts veiling it and preventing it from reaching its full glory. Islam used both hands to remove the cumbersome garment, sliding it down his thighs, then gave a kick that sent it hurtling through the air.

Captain Ni'mat, his gaze having followed that airborne trajectory, looked back to what the shorts had left in their wake and, heart racing, marveling, trembling, he whispered to himself: Oh the Manifold Splendor!

As if it had unfurled in a single movement, a single flight, a single illumination!

And though a mighty broadsword was the first to appear, cleaving the air with one slanted blow, the most beautiful of pistils emerged from that rent, quivering at first, then more assertive, slowly blooming, bursting with somber brilliance, and the terrible sword in its slanted rigidity and the supple pistil, alive, in bloom, were nonetheless made of the same atoms, the same matter, the same flesh, beauty one and the same, and Captain Ni'mat was on his knees, trembling knees, like an orant, before this unveiled beauty. Rapt over the Manifold Splendor that had already been revealed to him in his dream, when a miraculous archer, radiant in his nudity, had liberated him from menacing azure beings, revealed to him twice, for after that dream, wandering into the garden to cool off on that not-so-long-ago night, he had found it—the captain found it again—but that time the vision was tangible, confirmed by the moonlight bathing the hut in which slept an adolescent boy whose body appeared to be emitting radiations. And now, in this magical moment, the Manifold Splendor promised him was unfurling in plain day, and Captain Ni'mat reeled from joy, from gratitude, and at the same time, he felt sad and ashamed, more than anything, he felt terribly ashamed.

He was ashamed of the miserable, horrible piece of oiled, translucent plastic that he was holding in one trembling hand. Love in the time of the plague was forcing him to do something that was an insult to love, an attack against the Manifold Splendor.

Zohar! The Zohar a.k.a. the Book of Splendor! He suddenly realized that the phrase his lips continued to whisper—while with two trembling hands, he covered the tip of Islam's penis and began to unroll the condom onto his rock-hard member—was almost the exact title of a sumptuous Kabbalistic work, composed circa 1300 by Moses de León, in Granada, in a tolerant, learned, and playful Andalucía. Zohar! Splendor! The arrow of violence and love now had its head hooded and its body sheathed. Ready to run him through.

The amorous vassal having readied the war weapon of his young and very recent master, who now wielded the power of life and death over him, Captain Ni'mat lay down on his stomach at Islam's feet, hands in a cross like a recumbent statue, legs spread as wide as they could go, and, eyes closed, he assented with his whole body, his whole soul, to his new condition, to his new destiny.

For the first time, he assumed what he had become without shame, daring to say it, to whisper it to himself like the most beautiful of names: *Khawala!*

But when the Nubian archer unceremoniously entered him, that whisper abruptly, seamlessly, transformed to cries soon followed by groans and gasps, and then, beneath the final barrage of arrows released, by parturient howls and this supplication: "Islam, stop for a second. Stay inside me, but don't move."

The captain had barely recovered and begun to appreciate this lull when a sudden, rageful bucking prompted a new howl as he groveled belly down, repeating his plea. Islam, at the cusp of orgasm, kept going anyway. He, who like all the boys in his village had been initiated to sexual pleasure through bestiality upon reaching puberty, and after which never had any sexual outlet apart from masturbation, was so overcome by this profusion of flesh so fully offered to him that the captain's groans and screams of pain merely aroused him further. At the cusp of ejaculation, his tumescent penis, now hard as ebony wood, provoked such intense screams in Captain Ni'mat that Islam covered his mouth with one hand, pressing down against his entire body, long enough for him to finish inside the captain, with three deep and final jerks.

When his mouth was finally free, Captain Ni'mat was able to catch his breath, which was labored at first, then slowly calmed. Stretched out, or rather spread out, collapsed beneath a body in all the ardor of its youth, which, after irrigating him with its spring sap, remained planted in him like a tree, he was nothing but softened earth, the lukewarm humus of the undergrowth, larva plunged into a happy, blissful—blessed?—half-sleep.

The captain was pulled from this distant realm of silence, peace, and stillness by a rigidity he felt building inside him once again. Islam resumed his drilling movements, but his ever-ardent thrusts no longer hurt. Like a river that eventually carves itself a bed, Islam's penis had already created and widened a passage, of its exact dimensions, into which it was now fluidly, naturally, slipping. The jerky thrusting gave way to slow rhythmic pushing, simultaneously firm and gentle, to which Captain Ni'mat responded in perfect synchronization, lifting his buttocks when the rider astride him drew back his penis, and lowering it during the inverse motion. This choreography hit its crescendo when the two naked, interlaced dancers climaxed. For Captain Ni'mat, the profound joy of being sodomized mixed with that, at nearly the same moment, of a powerful ejaculation, creating an overwhelming, twofold orgasm. The waves of this twin pleasure spread throughout his body, which was literally climaxing through every pore. The pleasure was so new and troubling and intense that happy tears came to his eyes. As sometimes happened to his wife, when she orgasmed, he suddenly thought, but that was such a long time ago, when they were still young and she used to call him her falcon. This thought provoked neither shame nor unease in him. Nor did the realization that he had been sodomized by a teenager who was surely about the same age as his eldest daughter. Quite the opposite, the captain told himself that out of ignorance, respect for social conventions, and fear, he had deprived himself of a pleasure which he would never get enough of now in the years that remained to him to explore, like a continent, its geology and every landscape.

It was early July, and already summer had taken hold in all its splendor. Nearly one year had passed since Captain Ni'mat had begun his exploration.

2

CAPTAIN NI'MAT'S BLINDING REVELATION had come so late that the crucial matter of his age struck him acutely. Though his young Nubian lover responded to and satisfied his every desire, he nonetheless wondered whether affection, if not to say love, played any role at all in that willingness. If there was any affection or love to be found, it was inevitably tainted by venality, for Captain Ni'mat had tripled his servant's wages and showered him with gifts. Would other young house-boys who worked in the neighborhood also welcome his advances if he were to offer them a substantial monetary recompense? He bitterly regretted the single and rather foolhardy attempt he had made in that regard, which, though expressed ambiguously, had been met by a categorical refusal from the young man being solicited.

Captain Ni'mat naturally began to pay more attention to his appearance, a consideration seemingly completely forgotten by his compatriots. In his case, this
manifested as new sartorial choices, intensive physical
exercise, and, still related to the body, more discreet,
specific, and intimate rituals. For example, he now
periodically shaved his armpits, pubis, upper thighs,
perineum, and between his buttocks, spraying these
areas with a brand-name deodorant after each of the
three or four showers he took daily. His buttocks were
always exposed, even when he was dressed. When he
put on his briefs, the captain would fold and bend the
part of the fabric meant to cover his rear in such a way
that it formed a slender cord that conformed perfectly
to the cleft parting his buttocks. This idea of wearing his briefs like thongs had struck him as a way to
maintain a corporal, tangible, and tactile awareness
of what he had become and wanted to fully assume.
Deep down at least, mentally and physically, for in the
society in which he lived, it was out of the question to
publicly admit to being a homosexual.

As for his marriage, he and Mervet now slept in
separate bedrooms. The only times he visited her bed
were the days when he reached the peak of that dual
pleasure Islam procured for him and which brought
tears to his eyes. And though on those days he would

sleep with his wife, it was more for assurance, psycho-
logically, that he hadn't been completely feminized,
than out of any real desire. Mervet didn't take any true
pleasure either from these intermittent, increasingly
rare lovemaking sessions. On one occasion, Captain
Ni'mat realized that his virility was lacking, a failing
that recurred the next time. Neither Captain Ni'mat
nor Mervet viewed this impotence as catastrophic or
tragic. In fact, the captain saw it as an opportunity,
the ideal moment, to suggest to his wife that they keep
separate bedrooms, using her worsening snoring as an
excuse. When he left his wife's bed, it wasn't without
genuine albeit pointless remorse, as it had already been
one year since he himself had consummated something
akin to new nuptials.

Now, when he surrendered himself, though quite
infrequently, onto Abu Hassan's raised massage bed,
between the masseur's muscular hands and legs, he almost felt like he was being unfaithful to his young Nubian lover with whom he was practically in a conjugal
relationship.

Mervet wasn't blind, and she grew increasingly
curious about the change in her husband's behavior
toward their servant. He spoke informally to Islam,
sometimes in ambiguous language, a code known to
them alone, frequently patted him on the shoulder with

visible tenderness, and sometimes smiled at him in a very odd way. That complicity and gentleness, along with the solicitous and reciprocated interest she noticed in their exchanges, led her to suspect the horrible thing that, though she refused to call it by its name, nevertheless fueled her imagination and tortured her soul. If her husband was engaging in abhorrent sexual relations, then at least let it be as the man, in the dominant position. Such was her desperate hope if this curse had indeed entered her home. But if the father of her children, her falcon, was pursuing his forbidden love in the passive position, as the submissive partner, this would, in her mind, be a humiliation that rendered death preferable to life. For in the society in which she lived, like all Arab societies, the contemptuous Egyptian term *khawala* referred specifically and solely to the sexual partner being ridden. As for the rider, though he could be the object of reprobation, he was nonetheless not viewed with contempt. He remained a man, and even among the most virile of men, for another could serve as his mount, or spread out at his feet like a mop.

And so Mervet prayed that God spare her falcon this unforgivable degradation, this extreme humiliation, this unredeemable defeat. For if such a defeat had occurred, it would upend their marriage more radically than that endured by Egypt during the Six-Day War, which had resulted, three months later, in her husband's expulsion from the air force. If, in his twilight years and this time of his own accord, he had accepted this second, terrible defeat, she would quite simply expulse him from her life. The falcon—an affectionate nickname and august image spontaneously chosen by a young girl in love—would prove to be the most beautiful and cruelest of lies.

Mervet felt tortured and wanted to know the truth.

She heard it from one of her two closest friends, Chaïma. Or at the least, she was guided onto a path where the veil of doubt had been ripped away, and at the end of which she saw the black and blinding sun of truth rise.

Chaïma used circumlocutions and digressions to tell her unhappy friend what she had learned. First, without any ado, she announced that she was going to fire Mustapha, her household servant: "You know that he and Islam are thick as thieves. They're from the same village."

"Yes, but what did he do?"

"It's nasty gossip. He told me things I'm ashamed to repeat to you."

"You know perfectly well that you can tell me anything, Chaïma."

"It's just that it's so awful I can't put any stock in it. On the other hand, if it's all lies, I wonder what good it would do him to spread them."

"Come on, Chaïma, stop beating around the bush. It's not fun for me or you."

"Fine! So Mustapha, even though I'm sure the miserable wretch is lying, claims that your husband made him shameful propositions."

"Ni'mat?"

"Yes, but the worst of it is that, still according to Mustapha, when he told Islam about it, Islam said that Ni'mat had made him the same proposition one year ago now and that ever since..."

Chaïma stopped talking, shaking her hands in denial.

Mervet lost her temper and shouted: "For the love of God, tell me what you came here to tell me, however bad it is."

"Mervet, I hope you'll be strong as you confront this terrible situation. Here it is: according to what Islam told Mustapha, he and Ni'mat have been doing the horrible thing for almost a year."

Mervet went pale, raised her hands to the sky, and spun in a circle, as though overcome with dizziness. Then, back slumped, felled by the news, she went to the couch, where she collapsed. Chaïma sat beside her and affectionately clasped her hands.

"Don't let yourself be beaten down, Mervet. You need to make sure that this all isn't just a horrible lie, made up by either Mustapha or Islam."

"What reason would they have to spread such a lie?"

Chaïma admitted that the same question had been troubling her, adding: "What's more, Mustapha said that he decided to tell me because Ni'mat recently made him the same proposition again, and he didn't want to commit an act odious to God."

"Wait, so he's a *barbu*?"

In Egypt, as in most Arab countries, the term *barbu*—literally, bearded man—refers to members of the Muslim Brotherhood, but also by extension to all those of the Islamist persuasion.

"I don't think so. But lately he has been doing his five daily prayers regularly. It could very well be that the local 'brothers' have begun his indoctrination."

"That only gives more weight to what he dared confide in you."

Tears rose to Mervet's eyes and she began slapping her face, gently at first, then harder and harder, moaning as though she'd lost a loved one. Chaïma trapped her friend's hands in her own, promising she would get to the bottom of things by warning her servant of the serious trouble he'd be in if it turned out he had been telling lies.

"What's the point, Chaïma, now that doubt has worked its way into my mind like a poison? Good God, what'll become of us if this rumor circulates through the neighborhood?"

"It won't, trust me. Mustapha swore on the Koran that apart from him and Islam, nobody else knows."

"God damn the both of them, and their village, and their cursed Nubia."

"It's already done, for Nubia," noted Chaïma, daring a shy, sad smile, "submerged by the flood and all…"

"Ha! Before that damned pharaoh who changed Egypt and its history, back in the time of kings and pashas, a servant who dared spread such horrors about his masters, even if they were true, would have been castrated or had his lips cut off, or, if they were feeling merciful, he would have been forced to swallow red peppers by the handful until his mouth was on fire."

Suddenly, Mervet, downcast, stopped naming these harsh, delectable tortures to confess to her friend: "Now that I think about it, maybe those beasts Mustapha and Islam were telling the truth. I've noticed some rather shifty things lately. What can I do, Chaïma?"

Her friend and confidante thought for a moment, then laid out her idea. "Listen, Mervet, don't do anything. There are only two weeks between now and Ramadan. If Ni'mat truly did give in to satanic temptations, the month of fasting, the ideal time for contemplation and penitence, will be his only opportunity to get his act together. Why don't you suggest spending the month in Mecca? There's a good chance that making the Umrah pilgrimage during this sacred period will lead him to give up his degrading sexual practices, which, by the way, we still don't have undeniable proof of."

"It's a sensible plan, Chaïma, but you know that Ni'mat has never been very religious and that he thinks that the fastidious, diffuse, and oppressive atmosphere of religiosity that permeates our current society has nothing to do with true faith, which, in his eyes, can only be personal, interiorized."

"I know, but ask him anyway. Maybe he'll view it as a lifeline miraculously being offered to him."

"I'll try, Chaïma, but I don't expect much."

"Who knows? In any case, Mervet, it's the time to be brave. And most importantly, to keep your spirits up."

The two friends exchanged a warm hug and Mervet went all the way to the villa gate with this close confidante to whom chance had assigned the thankless role of messenger of damning news.

As Chaïma walked away, Mervet saw Islam approaching from the opposite direction. Bobby, scampering in a zigzag beside the boy, jumped at her once their eyes met. When he rose on his hind legs in front of her, canines gleaming with joy, she pet him affectionately and, casting a dark glance at the Nubian youth via whom scandal had perhaps already entered her home, whispered to her beloved dog: "Oh, if only you could rip him apart with those fangs!"

3

QUITE UNEXPECTEDLY, it was Captain Ni'mat who, the day after Chaïma and Mervet's conversation, asked his wife, "What do you think of an Umrah to Mecca, during the month of Ramadan?"

The suggestion came so opportunely, almost miraculously, that Mervet, surprised and delighted, couldn't contain her joy. "That's wonderful, Ni'mat! Seeing how long I've been wanting you to go with me, at least once, to the blessed, holy sites."

"The thing is, my dear Mervet, as agnostic as I believe myself to be, I think it will be a spiritual experience that can only prove beneficial for a man of my age. Several of my friends have told me that the pilgrimage was a decisive turning point in their lives."

"I'm happy to hear you say that, but isn't it a bit late for it?"

"No, I already talked to the director of a travel agency who said he could get us a very comfortable villa, one that belongs to some Saudi friends working abroad."

"Well then! That's perfect. I'm going to let Umm Hani know so she can watch the house while we're gone."

Umm Hani had worked for them for more than two decades and had become like a member of the family. When she reluctantly retired, crippled by rheumatism, their two daughters were already pursuing their studies abroad and the captain and his wife decided that hiring a new housemaid was unnecessary. The young Nubian, whom Captain Ni'mat had unearthed in Kom Ombo during a trip to Aswan, performed his various duties so well that there was no cause for complaint. Until Chaïma's shocking disclosure, which led Mervet to regret the departure of Umm Hani, who was now entrusted to care for the villa each time they traveled.

The first reason that Captain Ni'mat had the idea to spend Ramadan with his wife in Mecca had nothing to do with religion. He knew that during this month, it was out of the question that Islam provide him with the most intimate of massages, what they too called *attad-lik al hamimi* between themselves, even after breaking fast. For Islam, and even for Captain Ni'mat, agnostic though he was, that would have been the greatest of transgressions. But also, the captain was beginning to feel anxious about the potentially serious consequences of his quest for new partners to satisfy his desires. He had once again propositioned, quite unambiguously this time, Mustapha, who had repeated his initial indignant refusal and then recounted the incident to Islam. That in itself wasn't too worrying, but it could become so if Mustapha were also to tell his other friends. Not too long ago, the police had raided one of the boat-nightclubs berthed on the Nile, rounding up fifty or so men who were accused of sodomite practices and brought to court. Homosexuality was viewed as an extreme, serious perversion that challenged the foundations of religion and society, and a slanderous insult to the virility of Egyptian men. Some of the defendants were further accused, in a surrealistic conflation, of satanic crimes and collaboration with Israel!

The hunt for homosexuals could create endless problems for a man like Captain Ni'mat, who had served in the institution charged with defending the country.

These were the rational, secular considerations motivating the captain's plan to perform Umrah. The spiritual argument, the one he used with his wife, had arisen second, but there was undeniably still some truth to it. This motivation was rooted in one of the oldest, most established, and most attested traditions in Muslim culture, a tradition that can prompt a man or a woman immersed in such an environment since birth to one day decide to set foot on the ground where the prophet Mohammed preached. There were countless enlightening stories of people who had never bothered with religion, some even leading truly debauched existences, for whom the pilgrimage to the holy sites had been an awe-inspiring experience that radically changed their lives. Islamic inculcation is so deep and so tenacious, particularly in childhood, that many agnostics and even atheists will confide that listening to certain famous readers recite psalms from the Koran moves and shakes them to their core.

And so on the eve of the month of Ramadan, Captain Ni'mat "prepared his caravan," to borrow an ancient Bedouin expression that remains current, almost canonical in such circumstances, to fly with his wife to the holiest site in Islam. On the plane, thinking of his young lover from whom he would be separated for a month, he realized for the first time that the houseboy's name added an additional transgressive element to the relationship that had developed between them. And he sincerely hoped that his trip to Mecca would be a genuine spiritual experience that would give him new perspective on the other, deeply affecting but increasingly dangerous, experience, in which he had been participating for one year.

As for the captain's partner, Islam would find himself in the hands of someone who wished to put an end to their illicit affair: his friend Mustapha, whose indoctrination had borne fruit. The boy was now a true member of the Muslim Brotherhood. The circumstances—Captain Ni'mat's absence and the sacred month of fasting and penitence—could not have been more favorable to Mustapha's plan to guide his lost friend onto the right path. He easily convinced Islam to accompany him to the mosque every day, at first only for the five canonical prayers, but subsequently for the supererogatory prayers whose merits he explained. A daily reading of the suras of the Koran were of course part of what Mustapha viewed as a veritable quest of redemption for his poor friend. He returned several times to the verses about the people of Loth and the fiery destruction of the depraved city of Sodom.

Islam had no choice but to express agreement with what his friend was saying, but at night, when he lay down on his mattress, his thoughts turned to the absent captain. The most vivid images that came back to him were those in which his master, whom he had so feared at first, became a man who would sometimes cry from pleasure in Islam's embrace. Each time he recalled this metamorphosis from authoritative master to mere flesh, which he would knead, shape, and lash as he liked, Islam was overcome by a dizzying feeling of power, reinforced by and integrated into the generic, social contempt in which the *khawala* is held. But it was immediately joined by a hint of filial respect, of pity for this man his father's age, who had so belatedly become a slave to an irrepressible desire, and also by admiration for the courage shown by this captain who had dared remove the mask of authority and respectability to reveal himself, literally, naked and unique. Here, Islam, unawares, was touching upon the notion of the individual, the emergence of whom was opposed by everything in the society in which he lived. Looming over these mixed-up, contradictory feelings flooding his heart was the clear, monolithic discourse, founded on the authority of the holy word, delivered by Mustapha, the self-appointed director of Islam's conscience. And yet this discourse didn't keep Islam from reliving in his dreams, during this month of Ramadan, almost every other night, a love affair, damned by heaven, with the man who had perhaps gone to Mecca to free himself of its grip. Was it possible, Islam would think upon waking, that the captain was having similar dreams in the most sacred place on earth? But he quickly chased that sacrilegious question from his mind, cursing its certain instigator, Satan. He would then think of the outcome toward which he and the captain were perhaps heading, which was quite simply an end to a relationship condemned by man and God. But then self-interest—sordid, materialistic self-interest—inevitably reared its ugly head, and took the floor. If their sexual relationship ended, would Captain Ni'mat continue to be as generous with him? He had given Islam a completely new wardrobe, bought him the espadrilles manufactured by the brand collectively endorsed by the world's youth, a cell phone so he could call his mother in Kom Ombo whenever he wanted, and satisfied his every desire. Of course these changes hadn't gone unnoticed by Islam's peers, and certainly not by the perceptive Uncle Samir, who no doubt harbored his own ideas about their origin but, as usual, kept them to himself. The other individual intrigued by these changes, up until her intuition was confirmed by her friend Chaïma, had of course been Mervet.

And so Islam, all cleaned up, sporting brand-name shoes and thin, brightly colored summer garments, walked to the mosque every day of the month of Ramadan with Mustapha. Though his friend told him it would be more befitting to wear a humble and proper jalabiya, instead of the clothes he had obtained through his venal relations, Islam wouldn't concede on how he dressed. He had rediscovered a pride in his appearance that seemed to have been forgotten by the majority of his compatriots. Mustapha, the young, austere inquisitor, realized that his friend's redemption would take longer than he had thought.

As for Captain Ni'mat, deep within a human tide swelling with fervor, his mind frequently, involuntarily, filled with lascivious sexual images starring a young lover whose very name contained terribly transgressive undertones in this place. His musings about beauty—divine epiphany or carnal human temptation?—whose author, libertine or mystical, remained unknown to the captain, would then come back to him, whispered aloud like a prayer.

4

NEITHER CAPTAIN NI'MAT'S monthlong stay in Mecca
nor Islam's regular visits to the mosque during that
same period, nor his friend Mustapha's daily sermons,
prevented temptation from growing even stronger.

It happened ten days after Captain Ni'mat's return
from the Umrah, at the height of summer. By dawn, the
sweltering, stifling August sun had begun casting its
bright rays. At night, the panting earth would try to
catch its breath, expelling from its guts the heat it had
stored up during the day.

On one of these suffocating August nights, the captain, tormented by the heat and insomnia, went to the
villa garden for some air. Islam, bare-chested at the
entrance to his hut, seemed to be waiting for him. In
reality, he too was simply seeking a breeze, as slight
as it was. Each of the two lovers appeared to the other

like a ghost. Heart racing, Captain Ni'mat advanced toward this nocturnal, impromptu rendezvous. Once he reached Islam, he gave the boy a long look, then squeezed him tightly in his arms. When the captain released his silent embrace, Islam, also without saying a word, took him by the hand like a child, brought him into the hut, and shut the door behind them.

Neither found it necessary to speak. When Captain Ni'mat, who had removed the sole garment covering him, a light jalabiya made of thin fabric, moved to lie down on the mattress, Islam stopped him and stood behind him. Taking off his shorts, he began to rub his penis against the cleft of the captain's buttocks with one hand while the other traveled up his back applying increasing pressure. When Islam got hard, Captain Ni'mat felt the unsheathed sword ready to run him through, and the firm and commanding pressure of the hand on his shoulder told him what his young master and lover wanted. He bent over, spread his legs wide, and pressed the palms of his hands against the wall. The bucking motion that then shook him was so strong that his head almost rammed into the wall. But once he had been penetrated in this savage way, the penis that had bored its path with a single motion began to move gleefully with firm, though slow and gentle, thrusts, a regular, warm throbbing, ever more erect and gradually hardening, a gentle, loving hardness. Captain Ni'mat's flesh liquefied, evaporated, all that remained was gratitude for this loving, sublime act of sodomy that, bringing him to the peak of dual pleasure, made him ejaculate at the very same moment that his glorious rider came inside him, squeezing his thighs and pulling him closer.

Captain Ni'mat's knees continued to shake once he stood up. He was so overcome by joy that he felt no surprise when he heard someone knock violently at the hut door. To Islam's panicked motions, urging him to lie on the mattress and hide beneath the blanket, he merely responded with a bitter, vanquished smile. Then, pulling on his jalabiya, he slowly went toward the door and opened it.

Mervet's eyes cast murderous rays at him. She next directed them against Islam, then, without saying a word to either, she returned to the villa with a determined step.

Captain Ni'mat, emerging from the hut, suddenly felt like a stranger, an intruder, in this garden fragrant with roses. He raised his eyes to the sky. It was strewn with a profusion of sparkling, silent, and indifferent stars.

He felt like screaming, but no sound came from his mouth. He looked at Islam, now standing beside him as if seeking his protection, almost with surprise, as if he didn't recognize him.

For one week now, Mervet has maintained a state of silence from which she refuses to emerge. She barely eats and has grown shockingly thin. When I speak to her, she responds with a haggard expression, her large black eyes fixed on mine in a mute, terrible interrogation. She doesn't seem to hear what I'm saying. After the night I heard violent knocking on the door to Islam's hut, filled with that strange serenity that comes when you're confronted by the inevitable, it took me two days to be able to look her in the eyes again and stammer out an incoherent string of words to try to explain something that remained, to a large extent, inexplicable to myself. I told her repeatedly, as gently as I could, and overcome by sincere emotion, that if there was anyone in the world who could understand and forgive me, it was her. But all my pleas failed to get a word out of her, or bring a gleam of light to her widened eyes, which appeared to be contemplating an unfathomable abyss.

Is this the debut of a serious depression or is she already deep in its throes? Her sole reaction came, though still without a word, when I told her she should see a psychiatrist to get help overcoming the trauma she'd endured. She began to nod violently, while giving me a hard, unforgiving look.

I don't know what else to do, or rather I do, but I haven't dared yet. What I should have done first, and this is perhaps what my wife was expecting from me, was dismiss the person who brought on this scandal. But that decision has been heart-rending for me, and I've put it off from day to day. For I now fully recognize, and dare to name, without shame, in the deepest parts of myself, the feelings I have for Islam. It's quite simply love. And I should have renounced it, to bring back to life the frozen statue that is my wife, the woman with whom I shared the best years of my life.

As for Islam, the day after Mervet discovered us together in the hut, he told me he could never again look her in the eyes and that he had to leave the villa. I couldn't stop myself from affectionately stroking his hair when I saw the sadness darkening his ordinarily smiling face. I eventually convinced him, with difficulty, to wait a few more days.

In the expectation of what miracle?

God, dear God, why did you create bewitching beauty and then, at the same time, order us not to succumb to it and to worship you alone?

III

Kom Ombo

O Death, old captain, time to make our trip!

This country bores us, Death! Let's get away!

Even if sky and sea are black as pitch

You know our hearts are full of sunny rays!

BAUDELAIRE, "VOYAGING"

1

CAPTAIN NI'MAT, lacking anyone he could talk to about the inextricable situation in which he had gotten himself, sat down in his office that day and placed his head in his hands, not knowing what else to do. Suddenly, the sight of the luxury pen that his wife Mervet had given him long ago grabbed his attention. It seemed to him, for a fleeting moment, that the thin golden rings rimming the pen's beautiful black lacquer surface, at the ends and in the middle, were shining even more intensely. He took this as an invitation, in the absence of a human being in whom to confide, to again use this pen, a mere decorative object for some time now, and confide to the page all that was troubling his heart, his soul, and last but not least, his senses.

He took the pen from the attractive stand it had come with, and in which it had been stuck at an angle, lovingly stroked it as he thought of those distant, serene days when his wife had given him this gift for his birthday, removed the cap, and happily noted that the ink in the cartridge hadn't dried up but flowed easily as soon as he set the first words to the paper:

For one week now, Mervet has maintained a state of silence from which she refuses to emerge...

As the meditation about beauty, whose provenance — Sufi or libertine — he still didn't know, once again entered his mind, and just as he put it in writing, he heard someone knocking on the villa door, which he grudgingly rose to open. Chaïma, his wife's close friend, had come to inquire about her. Captain Ni'mat nodded sadly and invited the visitor, whom he also considered a close friend, to accompany him first to his office. There, he initially debated using vague and prudent circumlocutions to make their mutual friend understand the shock his wife had endured and the listless state in which she now found herself. But then, glimpsing the still-wet ink staining the page to which he had a few moments earlier confided his torments and doubts, he came to a wild decision. If he couldn't share the tragic and strange joy that had erupted into his life at this late age with one of his and his wife's oldest and closest friends, then what was the point of friendship? Without a word, looking into Chaïma's eyes, calm and determined, he held out the page he'd just written. She began to read in silence, her forehead tightening as she progressed. When she was done, she looked at her old friend with tear-filled eyes, and not a single sound emerged from her throat. Captain Ni'mat couldn't see what he could add after sharing, in writing, such an intimate, unambiguous confession. An oppressive feeling of unease set in, which might have persisted if a ghostly silhouette hadn't suddenly appeared in the office doorway. It was Mervet, in a white jogging suit, hair undone, face emaciated, eyes inordinately wide. Chaïma rose swiftly, hands extended, and rushed to her now unrecognizable friend. Warmly taking Mervet into her arms, Chaïma kissed her on the cheeks as she affectionately stroked her hair. But to her great surprise, Mervet had no reaction to this show of compassion and friendship. After a moment during which she remained as still as a statue, she turned around without a word and moved like a sleepwalker toward her bedroom, which had in truth become a cell in which she remained confined most of the time.

"I would be so grateful to you, my dear friend, if you could get Mervet to talk."

It was Ni'mat, with a dejected voice, who was asking this favor of their mutual friend.

Chaïma nodded sadly and headed toward the cell where she found the recluse lying on her bed, her inordinately wide eyes staring at the ceiling as if at an abyss dug beneath her feet. Chaïma sat beside Mervet on the edge of the bed, took her hands in hers, again tenderly stroked her hair, then, after a long moment spent in this friendly and silent communion, tried to find and say some words of comfort.

"This will pass, my dear, it will pass. We'll get through this difficult ordeal together. Don't let it bring you down like this, sweetheart…"

But these words of comfort and encouragement had no effect on Mervet, who didn't look away from the ceiling abyss and into her friend's eyes until Chaïma thought it worth adding: "The first thing we'll do is send that terrible animal that goes by the name of Islam back to his cursed Nubia."

It was only then that Mervet regained the use of her tongue, to say in a determined, savage voice: "No, no, no, neither he nor the man who called himself my husband exists anymore. They found their happiness in disgrace and depravity, so let them stay there. But to me, they no longer exist. They're two strangers who continue—can you imagine?!—to live under the same roof as me, I don't know why, or for how long."

One of the two men, the two strangers that no longer existed in Mervet's eyes, had heard everything, hidden near the door to the room of reclusion. Captain Ni'mat, abashed as a child and eyes misty with tears, went toward the bed where his wife was sitting up and giving him a hard stare. He kneeled at the foot of the bed, begging: "Darling, for the sake of the life we've shared for over forty years, of the joy and pain we've shared, of our two daughters and the grandchildren they'll soon give us, forgive me, forgive me."

Then, carried away by a surge of resuscitated tenderness, he delicately placed one hand on his wife's knees, the other holding the hand of their mutual friend, Chaïma, to whom he turned, still begging, seeking agreement in the place of alms.

"Isn't that right, Chaïma? That it would be absurd for such a long life together to be broken and reduced to nothing because of an affair I found myself involved in without knowing how, that forced itself on me, and that I in no way premeditated. Who can be assured that they'll go through life without some terrible, strange ordeal swooping down on them one day, with no warning, abruptly casting doubt on their every certainty and plunging them into a state of utter disarray? Try to understand, Mervet, and you too,

Chaïma, my sweet friend. Try to understand the disarray in which I found myself and don't condemn me
with no recourse!"

This plea was followed by a quickly suppressed sob
that shook the former war pilot's stocky body, as he
remained kneeling before two women from whom he
was requesting aid and understanding.

Chaïma's simple, human response to his call for
help came like a soothing balm: "Ni'mat, know that
I don't condemn you at all, and that if I was tempted
to act as your judge, our friendship would prevent me
from doing so."

Captain Ni'mat directed a look of gratitude at this
woman proving herself to be a true friend, then, noting
that Mervet was still giving him a hard and merciless
stare, he said: "Try to listen to your heart, Mervet darling. I'm not asking you to answer me right away. As
for me, I'm going this instant to let Islam know he's
been dismissed from this house."

At that, he rose, turned his back on the two women,
and resolutely went into the villa garden.

He found the future exile sitting on a small, low
stool, petting Bobby, who was lying in a semicircle at
his feet, visibly delighted by the attention. Had some
mysterious animal instinct let him intuit that these soft,
nimble fingers were petting him for the last time?

Captain Ni'mat stopped a few steps away from this scene of affection, beauty, and peace, which struck him as almost unreal.

When the young Nubian looked up, the captain beckoned him over. Bobby, strangely—or quite naturally, sensing that the inevitable had begun to unfold—didn't follow Islam and cast a doleful glance at the man who had summoned his playmate. That man was telling Islam in a whisper whose dire significance the dog's keen ear could nonetheless perceive and perhaps understand, with an understanding that went beyond language, "Son, I have to let you go."

Islam wasn't particularly surprised. He had been expecting this announcement and had already prepared for it, so he acquiesced with a nod, in silence.

"What do you plan to do?"

"I was thinking of going back to Kom Ombo, but there's no work there. Luckily, I got a job offer recently, just yesterday."

"Here, in Ma'adi?" asked Captain Ni'mat, his voice trembling slightly, from joy or dread, he wasn't sure.

He knew that his desires would continue to torture him if this young man sent by fate had found a new job in the same neighborhood. Islam's response provided partial relief.

"No, it's in Zamalek."

That was one of the chicest neighborhoods in Cairo, and Captain Ni'mat congratulated his former factotum (though that horrible term wasn't how he referred to Islam in his mind): "Well! That's perfect. I'm happy for you. By the way, you can always contact me if you need anything at all. Here, I'll write down my cell phone number for you."

Islam smiled, pointing out to his former master (and how did he refer to the captain, deep down?) that he knew his number by heart, then, smile vanishing, he added in a sad and serious voice, "Wouldn't it be better for you, Captain, to end all contact with me, even by phone?"

"Look, my boy, you never know. If you need something or if God forbid you have to deal with a serious problem, it's always good to have someone to talk to. How could I forget, and you too I hope, the moments of joy that we spent together? But from now on, think of me like an understanding, loving father that you can turn to at any time."

These words moved Islam to tears. But the code of virility and honor internalized in men, in virile males like him, in Arab-Muslim societies beginning in childhood, erected its immaterial, impenetrable iron dyke, and kept the tears of emotion from pouring forth, from falling freely on shimmering cheeks that they would have softened and relaxed.

The young Nubian finally told the man who had asked that he henceforth view him like a father: "You too. You have my cell phone number, and you can call me at any time. I will always be your faithful servant. I'm going to get my suitcase; it's already packed. Goodbye, Captain."

As Islam walked to his hut, Captain Ni'mat whispered in desperation, "Not goodbye, just until next time, my...," and without finishing the silent phrase tearing him up, he followed the fate-sent youth. Just as the captain reached the hut door, Islam came out, carrying the sad suitcase that contained all his material possessions.

Captain Ni'mat hugged him, and in a choked-up voice whispered in his ear, "You might have been my last battle in this life, and my ultimate defeat."

Then, after hugging him tightly once again, he released the boy, staring at him intensely, as if he wanted to hold on to him, and added: "And perhaps my last joy. Now go."

2

A FEW DAYS after dismissing the teenage boy who threw my life into upheaval, I hired a cleaning woman, as it was now out of the question that our house servant be a man, young or old. Islam's dismissal and his replacement by a woman, who went by Umm Samar, have contributed to my wife's recovery. Mervet is gradually starting to speak again, but she still hasn't shared her intentions regarding the fate of our marriage, which, in any case, I'm in no rush to learn, imagining the worst.

In the meantime, to avoid succumbing to crushing sorrow, and to clarify my own thoughts, I've decided to keep a diary in which I'll attempt to set down with utmost sincerity all that troubles the deepest, most secret corners of my mind. As soon as I made this decision, I realized how original, almost iconoclastic, it is in the society I live in. That's because this diary is a form of resistance to the collective—the "group"—and to a gossipy oral culture and its clichés. It's a way to affirm myself, as a unique, singular individual, individual and singular being notions almost entirely confined to the domain of things unthought, or even unthinkable, among the vast majority of my fellow Egyptians. Though not as transgressive as the love affair I carried on for one year, which I would no longer label as cursed, but indeed as singular, and which showed me a new form of happiness, keeping this diary also struck me as another way to assert my individuality against the collective and its norms.

The first question that came to me, which immediately convinced me that liberating oneself from this collective wasn't an easy or obvious thing to do, was as follows: why was it that in my twilight years, at an age when many of my compatriots— the "group" again—who never paid much attention to religious dictates, even blithely breaking them, are undertaking what they call arroujou' ila Allah, "the return to God," I myself, at the polar opposite of that "return," succumbed to a transformative love affair, condemned by heaven and man alike? If I'd never had that truly transformative experience, what side would I have found myself on, I suddenly, anxiously wondered, recalling the still quite recent arrests, on a boat-nightclub moored to the banks of the Nile, of fifty young men accused of indulging in the same kind of relationship that linked Islam and me for one year, and at that—aggravating circumstances—under my own conjugal roof? Would I have sided with the howling wolves, the relentless inquisitors, the professional conflators of things? Indeed, what weren't those poor young men accused of?! They insulted

Egyptian virility, weakened the moral fiber of the nation, and indulged not only in sodomite practices but satanic ones as well, encouraged in their perverse and subversive efforts by international Zionist propaganda! Nothing less than that, as proclaimed and wrote certain eminent "intellectuals" whose "good sense" should have kept them a thousand leagues from the wolfpack and its wild accusations. Lawyers, professors, journalists, and writers—in other words, the truly "elite," or the "intelligentsia," as they would have said back in the day. I've placed several words in quotation marks because their meaning has been completely perverted, and because that perversion of language is one of the major signs of crisis and disintegration within a society.

The confessions and criticisms I'm setting down in this diary could cost me dearly if it ever fell into the hands of one of those "intellectuals," that is, one of those new inquisitors whose ranks keep growing, but I accept that risk.

But exactly when will we finally attain the status of individuals who enjoy indissoluble rights that include, to start, the freedom to think as we like and to control our own bodies and sexual orientation?

Men like me, who have known a singular kind of love, are asked, and then ordered to respond: What are you doing to Arab virility, to our magnificent, admirable, and sacrosanct Arab virility?

Yes, that virility in its highest form, muruwwa, was the cardinal virtue of the Bedouin of the Arabian desert, perfectly suited to the free and savage life he led. Later, in the centuries when Arab civilization was at its zenith, that desert virility was polished by urban culture and refinement, equated to humanism by the adab. But now? We're not a dozen centuries but eons away from these two magical eras during which virility, in different forms, saw its grandest, most human expression. Our contemporary "virility" has taken the guise of naked strength, of domination of the strongest over the weakest, of the tyranny of power most often conflated with the chief—the zaïm, the supreme warrior, an über, virile male who terrorizes and feminizes his entourage and the entire society over which he dominates. It's hardly surprising, then, that these dominated, feminized males, who nonetheless continue to believe they still bear the blazing emblem of virility, engage, inebriated and enraged, in a savage, widespread, and limitless form of virility, from whom the first to suffer, with the theologians' blessing, are those who, according to the Chinese sages, "hold up half the sky"—women.

Well, mea culpa! I freed myself from that straitjacket that imprisons and binds us. I renounce, with no remorse, the savage and degraded virility whose code I obeyed for a good part of my life. Now that I think about it, wasn't the very choice of a career as a war pilot, a celestial falcon spitting fire over peaceful valleys and terrorized men, dictated in large part by that supreme ideal of virility? Sacrificing as a result the things that excited me and filled me with joy: literature, and learning new languages, starting with French, so soft and mellifluous, a language favored by our former aristocracy and which I, even though I came from a modest family, chose as my first foreign tongue. And so I truly understand my wife's despair and heartbreak when she realized her "falcon" had metamorphosed into…

And yet, in the golden age of Arab-Islamic civilization, a love for boys had its cachet, its appointed, famous poets, like Abu Nuwas, among others, whose libertine, melodious, and subtle verses were on everyone's lips. Homosexuality didn't only flourish in royal courts, but had spread widely to all social classes and strata. In a more subdued register, and today still, countless foreign observers have noted with surprise the "homosensuality" that colors male interactions in cafés, the hammam, and even the street, when they see two men walking side by side, hands interlaced or one's arm around the other's waist, like two betrotheds.

What our society in fact looked down upon, and still does to this day, is passive homosexuality. Active homosexuality wasn't considered as such, but on the contrary as resounding proof of virility—that notion again—that in no way degraded the individual who practiced it. He remained a Man, a male, a vir, a fahl, a "stud," whereas whoever allowed himself to be ridden, the khawala, was worth less than a dirty mop spread on the ground and was, is, subject to every insult.

What condemnation, what punishment would they inflict on me, an ex-soldier, if one day I had the courage to publish *this diary? If they learned that late in life, for one year, I was a pansy, a mop, that I belonged to those dregs of society and humanity that are the* khawalat, *the faggots? It would be taken as resounding confirmation of the link the judges of those fifty young detainees claimed to establish between homosexuality, satanism, and a diabolical Zionist enterprise intended to emasculate and feminize our society in order to dominate and subjugate it.*

A "falcon" of the sky metamorphosed into a khawala! *The forever bitter taste of the defeat of June 1967, my personal defeat and that of my entire generation, soldiers and civilians alike, rises in my throat. Could it be that those six fateful days in that sweltering month of June marked the first violent blow to my fortress of "virility" of which I was as proud, if not more so, as everyone else? A blow that opened a gaping breach inside of me, but in which my virility nonetheless remained tightly packed, embalmed, useless, until the day I encountered a singular kind of love, which is now allowing me to undo the bandages of the mummy I was unknowingly carrying within and expel his stinking corpse. Yes, the corpse of a virility that has become, in our society, nothing more than an impulse for domination and death.*

Let me return to my initial hypothesis, rewording it as follows. Is it possible that the stinging defeat of 1967, which I experienced as inadmissible, unacceptable impotence and an inexpiable regret, created in me a feeling of such agonizing guilt that, gnawing at me in silence, slowly but relentlessly, it led me, more than three decades after the traumatizing event, to aspire to a sort of strange redemption, by accepting in my flesh and body—and in my heart and soul too—that impotence? That feminization of the terribly vanquished warrior, on his knees, flat on his belly? Could my metamorphosis into a khawala be the extreme and desperate incarnation of my protest and revolt against a fantasized notion of virility, grandiose and empty rhetoric, and the tyranny and recklessness of the chief, the supreme male—all the things that led us to catastrophe and shame back then? Might drinking the chalice of that catastrophe and shame to the dregs, late in my life, be the strange and cruel redemption to which I've unconsciously aspired for so many years? If I had participated in the "immortal," "double" victory of October-Ramadan 1973, would the strange desire to be possessed by a young teenager never have taken hold of me? Though, when I picture in my mind my former companions in arms, who had the chance to participate in that "immortal" victory, and are now retired generals who spend most of their time at the Ma'adi club, gossiping and trading nuktas, I tell myself that in the end, I didn't lose out on much. They suddenly strike me as actual mummies frozen in a prestigious but bygone era, a dead era, whereas I, who have only ever known the bitter taste of defeat, am still alive. I managed to inspire if not love, then desire in a young and radiant teenage boy who made of my body a celebration—oh those unforgettable nights!

oh that double climactic peak that brought tears to my eyes just like my wife at the moment of orgasm!—a spring continuously blooming throughout one cycle of four seasons.

Of course I can't give total credit to this hypothesis of guilt and redemption that keeping this diary has allowed me to venture. In lieu of this primitive self-psychoanalysis, I should be embarking on a process of genuine psychoanalysis if I truly want to understand myself. But like so many other triumphs of modernity, does psychoanalysis have any meaning beneath our theological skies that thunder a single truth into us? The fact that eminent Egyptian psychoanalysts such as Jacques Hassoun and Mustapha Safwan chose to live and practice in Paris, certainly for different reasons, is nonetheless indicative of the nearly insurmountable difficulties that prevent the most precious triumphs of the mind and reason from taking root in the fertile ground of our brains and bodies. What's more, psychoanalytical treatment is an exhausting, long-term endeavor, which can last a number of years, and I don't have enough left to appreciate the eventual liberation such an endeavor would bring me. For that matter, do I truly want that "liberation"? Whatever the obscure, unconscious motivations of my strange desire may be, I fervently wish that its blaze be in no way extinguished. And I remain hopeful that it will illuminate the few years I have left to live.

A combination of elements—this sincere, liberated vein of introspection in which I'm indulging, the appeasement it is

*slowly but surely bringing me, the rehabilitation of a love con-
demned by society and that I now consider to be an integral, es-
sential part of what makes me a unique individual—convinced
me of the superficiality, triviality, reductionism, and crass
ignorance of the biological explanation: the hypersensitivity
of the "prostata" in older men as the cause of their feminization. Once again, with a painful lump in my throat, I thought
of those young men arrested in a nightclub and on whom the
judges forced a humiliating anal exam. They, like the masseur
at the Ma'adi club, Abu Hassan, no doubt also believed in a
natural, physiological cause for homosexuality. Would someone of my age, if I had the misfortune to be handed over to their
judgment, be prescribed an exam of the "prostata"? Would they
go so far as to order it removed, even if it didn't prove to be cancerous, given that, according to them, the subversive metastasis
that homosexuality spreads through the societal body is more
pernicious, and with greater consequences, than that of a true
cancer ravaging a single individual's body? Pushing aside this
nightmarish scenario, I thought of my prostate, not of course as
the causal factor for my "inversion," but as a gland that could
hypertrophy in a man of my age and indeed become cancerous.
At this thought, I was overcome with anxiety, and I promised
myself that I wouldn't wait any longer to get a voluntary, ratio-
nally motivated medical exam before, who knows and God forbid, an ignorant judge were to order the barbarous, irrevocable
removal of my prostate.*

Immersed in these thoughts, in this worry and anxiety, I was far from imagining that the true worry, the true threat, and the true anxiety that would beset me had already reached my threshold.

A nocturnal inquisitor had painted on my villa door, in blood letters: WE DON'T WANT ANY KHAWALAT IN OUR NEIGHBORHOOD.

"We": the Group. Which was ordering the singular individual that I wanted to remain to get out. But only of Ma'adi?

Wishing to reach the status of an individual, I realized in terror that the price I'd have to pay might prove exorbitant. I had to envisage the possibility of becoming a stranger, a pariah, not only in my childhood neighborhood, but perhaps also in this beautiful, vast, dirty, and miserable metropolis that we continue to call—don't we, my brother-enemies, my admirable, epicurean, intolerant, and chauvinistic compatriots?—Umm al Dunya, "the mother of the universe."

But how can one possibly imagine, with any courage and serenity, being expelled from the belly of such a "mother"?

3

It was Umm Samar, the recently hired cleaning lady, who, arriving early that morning, found the villa door splattered with red, still-fresh paint. Illiterate, she couldn't decipher what was written, and alerted Captain Ni'mat, whom she found in the garden playing with Bobby, who immediately bounded toward her for his morning walk.

Captain Ni'mat read the anonymous, threatening message in alarm and ordered Umm Samar to fetch a mop and bucket of water to clean up the filth. When she asked for an explanation, he responded with a white lie: "It's probably some bratty kids amusing themselves by spraying graffiti, imitating, yet again, Western teenagers. Rude little copycats!"

"May God steer them to the right path," Umm

Samar indulgently replied with a sigh, before beginning to vigorously clean the stained door.

When she was done, Captain Ni'mat gently but firmly told her: "And please, Umm Samar, not a word to hanem Mervet. You know how anxious and fragile she still is."

The housecleaner merely made the appropriate and conventional gesture for when one is asked to keep a secret: middle and index fingers joined, she sewed her lips shut with an imaginary needle and thread.

When she took out the dog, Captain Ni'mat, left alone, began to pace back and forth in the villa garden, absorbed by bitter musings. How many people had seen the vile message? Who had written it? The name Mustapha—to whom he had recklessly proposed, on two occasions, relations similar to those he had conducted with Islam—blazed across his mind. He grabbed his cell phone and called the number of his former factotum and lover. When the captain heard Islam's voice, he had the impression it was coming from an infinitely distant place and time, though the boy had only been gone roughly one month and was working in Zamalek, a neighborhood that you could reach from Ma'adi by car in under an hour. The emotional moment passed—would their paths cross again, following such a recent and devastating separation?—and Captain Ni'mat told Islam about the unfortunate incident and his suspicion that the boy's closest friend, Mustapha, must be the culprit. If that was the case, Islam was to warn him that if he did it again, Captain Ni'mat was still well enough connected that he could force him to leave not only the Ma'adi neighborhood, but the city of Cairo. There was also a more radical solution: throw him into some dark hole and ensure no one would hear of him for a long time.

When Islam hung up, after promising to speak to his friend to determine whether the captain's suspicions were founded, Ni'mat resumed his pacing, still lost in bitter thoughts. After having himself condemned, in his diary, the savage virility whose only remaining guise was force, power, and domination, what had he done but spontaneously resort to the same, issuing threats that he was in no position to make, much less carry out?

Thinking about Mustapha again, Captain Ni'mat anxiously wondered if the boy hadn't long transitioned from the stage of piety and prayer, leading others through example, to that of militant, radical Islamist engagement. In which case, and if he was behind the threatening message, the captain should expect forms of persecution much more serious than anonymous graffiti tagged overnight. A young fanatical Islamist would certainly resort to the most extreme measures, especially with the trial of fifty young men accused of sodomy still fresh in people's minds and continuing to arouse indignant protests, not only from Islamists but from all manner of inquisitors. And wasn't Captain Ni'mat a fitting target, deserving, due to his perverse practices, of an exemplary punishment?

The dread twisting the captain's heart at these somber ideas quickly ceded to another, less damning feeling: sadness. Poignant sadness, both gentle and entirely hopeless, for his now unrecognizable country, for the metamorphosis of his society that had led to the emergence of these packs vowing their murderous hatred of all who strayed from the norms of the collective, of anything that might mark an individual as unique, from his faith to his romantic choices. At this late stage of his life, Captain Ni'mat was realizing that he couldn't publicly assert his status as an individual. His sadness was all the more poignant when he thought about how even the person closest to him, who had shared his life, couldn't understand or admit this strange love that had swooped upon him, leaving him powerless. Societal intolerance, lack of understanding from those closest to him...what remained but to scream and revolt? Captain Ni'mat regretted having ordered Umm Samar not to tell his wife about the graffiti on their door. Why should he keep living a lie, with a wife gone nearly mute? If she could neither understand nor forgive him, what was the point of continuing to live together?

Walking with determination, Captain Ni'mat went to the bedroom in which Mervet had carved out her life as a recluse.

4

A MODEST APARTMENT in the working-class neighborhood of Al Fajjala is my home now, and where I'm reviving this diary that I began in a plush villa where I knew happiness before the event that disrupted my entire life.

Mervet finally made her choice. I went to her bedroom, full of anger and revolt that quickly subsided when I saw my wife's devastated, unrecognizable face. She let me talk without interruption for nearly an hour, during which I appealed to her heart at times, and her reason at others, to make her realize that a yearlong indiscretion couldn't reduce our forty years together to nothing. I resorted to the metaphor, bombastic I admit, of planetary disruptions, in an attempt to explain to her that what happened to me had been as abrupt and unpredictable as mudslides, earthquakes, and volcanic eruptions are to man. I invoked her love, our love, for which this was the ultimate opportunity to prove itself stronger than the screams and threats of the horde. Once I had exhausted all my arguments, Mervet gave me a long look, then responded simply: "What you're saying moves me, Ni'mat, but I've made my decision. It would be best for us that we divorce."

Her words chilled me at first, then, almost immediately, a feeling of indescribable liberation and strange, wonderful, and gratifying serenity filled my whole being. I stood and in a calm and poised voice, avoiding any hint of emotion, said: "If you like, we can go see the adouls today. After that, I'll leave the villa. I ask your forgiveness for what happened and I wish you all the happiness possible in this world."

My wife unconsciously lifted her hands toward me and was about to rise from her bed. Then she abruptly curbed that spontaneous impulse and nodded slowly, in a sign of acceptance of what I had said and which for that matter corresponded to what she wanted.

It was with sincerity that I wished my wife all the happiness possible during this brief goodbye. My departure could be the start of her healing. She had a villa at her disposal, would soon come into possession of her family's expropriated land, and what's more had close, trusted female friends who would help her through those difficult early days of solitude. I knew that I myself could no longer count on true friendship, the only kind that's worth anything, that doesn't ask you questions and accepts you the way you are, or that you've become. Because I knew that in the eyes of my best friends, namely my former companions in arms, I had become a sort of monster. And that in turn I would have to confront another, implacable monster: solitude.

I didn't choose a modest apartment buried in a working-class neighborhood solely for financial reasons, but also because I knew that I would be viewed as a pariah if I remained within my social circles. Not only had I relinquished my "virility," which, in the eyes of my compatriots, represents the essence of a man, I had also betrayed my class, its privileges, and its corresponding halo of authority for a "depraved" love affair with a servant.

The instant I set down that sentence, I felt hands as supple as vines and cool as dew cover my eyes. I took those hands and lovingly brought them, eyes closed, to my lips. And who else would those hands belong to, if not my young, returned lover who, with his elastic feline movements, had slipped into the kitchen where I was writing and placed himself behind me without my noticing?

After my chaste kiss, we left the kitchen and headed, by tacit agreement and without a word, toward the hard, narrow bed that came with this furnished apartment—our nuptial (royal!) bed—and which is now my consolation for all the humiliations and miseries of existence.

As soon as I moved to Al Fajjala, I realized that without Islam's company, I had no other way to escape my solitude and despair apart from suicide. So I called him, on a Thursday, and managed to convince him to come over the following day, which was his weekly day off, as is the case for most Egyptians.

He came by fairly late, around noon. Both of us aware of the transgressive nature of our reunion, we furiously made love as calls to Friday prayer by three or four muezzins spread through the sky over Al Fajjala and penetrated, slightly buffered, the dimly lit bedroom.

Islam had placed my feet on his shoulders and, kneeling, his two hands under my loins, he sodomized me firmly but gently, with slow thrusts, his penis burying itself deeper and deeper, gradually growing harder and harder, until it was hard as a sword tearing me apart, and I let out a torrent of moans. When Islam finally withdrew, his member had carved such a gulf within me that I immediately, uncontrollably, unbearably felt the need that he return at once to fill that intolerable gulf. I voiced that desire, that need, to Islam, who responded with all the understanding, gentleness, and ardor of which he was capable.

He lay down on his side and slowly turned me over so I was in the same position, my back to him. Soon enough I felt his now supple penis begin its preliminary caresses, granting the somber and secret lips of my body gentle kisses. I brought my hand to his member and helped him, incited him, to touch me harder, more passionately, more violently. Kisses may be exquisite, but only the reciprocal skirmishing and biting of tongues, of sexual organs—entailing, for me and Islam, a *marvelously paired sword and a sheath of flesh—can transport us to rapture and ecstasy. When I finally felt his penis, supple as a vine, suddenly harden in my hand, transforming into a cruel and violent sword just as I wanted, I gently impaled myself on the unsheathed weapon. Islam, still, allowed me to do as I pleased until he reached the cusp of orgasm. He then slowly began to turn onto his back, his hands around my stomach and the rotational movement of his body carrying mine with it, until we were both lying on our backs, him sprawled on the bed, me above him and his stela of flesh loftily erecting itself inside me. With my legs spread on either side of his, the palms of my hands flat against the bed, the gulf in my body, moving up and down and back and forth, impaled itself on that Nubian, granitic stela, whose texture, I thought to myself in a state of intoxication, was the same as the granite from which Luxor Temple and the giants of Abu Simbel had been sculpted and carved. Oh stela, hard and gentle! Oh stela, painful like a stake and soothing like a balm! Oh stela that's come alive, pulsating, transformed from obsidian to plant and flower, to white sap and golden pollen! Oh my vibrant, magical Nubian fruit, my spectacular Nubian offering!*

My soul satiated and my body at rest, lying on a carpet of flowers, my head on the pillow and turned toward that of the miraculous teenager whose loins were that flowered carpet, I looked at him, though who could say how? With gratitude? Amazement? Embarrassment before such impudent joy?

Muffled words from the impassioned speech being given by the imam in the nearest mosque penetrated our bedroom, flying over our nuptial bed, and the word "hell" was repeated often. We were now both stretched out on our backs, side by side, silent, the fingers of my lover's left hand interlaced with those of my right hand. The imam was talking about hell and Islam was tenderly caressing my fingers, one by one. At one point it felt like he had slipped an engagement ring onto each, differentiated by substance, texture, form, and color but all equally precious. Oh the splendor of my quintuple rings! Oh ruby and emerald and amethyst and all the rest, all mine, oh the diamond of the African night and the jade of the Middle Kingdom, oh fabulous treasures, oh insolent riches and munificent opulence!

I was a poor old forsaken woman whom a Prince Charming emerging from submerged Nubia had come to save from misery, solitude, decrepitude, and death.

After this amorous delirium, could I still call myself, including in my own mind, Captain Ni'mat? I was maddened by love, so much so that if someone had called me crazy one day, I doubt I would have blamed them. I might have been on the right path, in that quest for some strange redemption whose price was that I drink to the dregs the chalice of my defeat and shame. But were they mine alone?

After a prolonged silence in utter communion, we rose to wash up and eat something. As Islam was splashing his face with large sprays of water, I followed his movements in a daze, asking myself what this teenage boy meant to me in the end. My lover? My betrothed? The instrument of my shame and my redemption? Abruptly, I told him with—I could feel it—a tone of supplication as well as a note of hope: "Habibi, darling, don't you think it's really not enough to only see each other on Fridays, on your weekly day off?"

"What choice is there, Captain? I don't have a moment to myself the other days. I slave away from daybreak to the last evening prayer."

The response burst from my lips on its own, simple, clear, and distinct: "You just need to come live here with me."

My suggestion stunned Islam at first. He thought for a minute, then pointed out, "But we'll arouse people's suspicions again and you really don't need more trouble, Captain."

"We won't have any trouble if you don't tell anyone where you work, or the nature of our relationship. As for me," I added in a trembling voice, "I won't make any more propositions to anyone. I now know that you are and will be until my death my only love."

As great as Islam's affection and tenderness for me might have been, this declaration of boundless love inevitably shocked him, young manly creature that he was, raised from earliest childhood in a cursed, harmful cult of virility. It came as no surprise when I heard him ask, after a moment of reflection, and in a tone that revealed what disconcerted him about my proposal, "If I understood you correctly, Captain, what you're suggesting is that we live sort of like husband and wife."

"Exactly," I answered, adding, "It will be our precious, sacred secret. Everyone else will think you work for an old divorcé who puts you up. Another thing: no one in this neighborhood knows that I was once in the military. So no more 'Captain,' not when we're with other people, not when we're alone. You'll simply call me by my first name: Ni'mat."

"That'll be hard for me, Captain, but I'll try."

"Perfect. And don't be surprised if I call you Habibi from now on, instead of Islam."

Was it that term of affection that broke the last dikes, sweeping away any remaining hesitation? My young lover's golden mouth rewarded me with these words: "If it will make you that happy, Captain…I mean, if it will bring you joy, Ni'mat. I owe it to you, after everything you've done for me."

"Only from obligation?" I asked him. "So you don't love me even a little?"

Islam simply made a gesture common among Egyptians, which consists of pointing your middle and index fingers at your eyes, almost touching them, thereby signifying that the person you're addressing is as dear and precious to you as the pupils of your eyes.

"Is that true?" I insisted, though his gesture had filled me with joy.

His only response was to take me by the hand like a child and guide us—oh third grace on this Venusian day—toward what would truly become our nuptial bed. On which the child I had been just a moment prior would soon, again, metamorphose into an old madwoman crazed with joy and happiness.

The very evening of that Friday blessed between us, Islam moved in.

Life was wonderful, and worth living.

Every day and every night my young lover made a celebration of my body…

He never had the luxury of watching pornographic movies, hadn't read Sheikh Nefzaoui's manual of erotology, The Perfumed Garden, *or the* Kama Sutra, *but Islam invented for our naked bodies pairings, weldings, solderings, jointings, and mountings equal to the greatest and most baroque of erotic architectures. Where did he find his inspiration for this consummate art of lovemaking? This unprecedented form of pleasure? When I asked him the question one day—I was in the "folded leaf" position, the leaf blade formed by his body blanketing and clinging to the leaf blade formed by my body, from its most delicate innervations to its most visible—his response, which he only gave after our joined leaf blades unfolded and again unfurled on our respective sides, stunned me.*

"*You're the first human being I've made love to.*"

Though this admission brought me the joy one would imagine, I couldn't help but reflect about how such sexual frustration could, like the sleep of reason, produce monsters. I thought about the women captured by the young emirs of the jihad that long raged in Algeria and the fate reserved them: either disembowelment (or throat slitting) or rape theologically justified as marriage, though oftentimes the two abominable acts succeeded one another and murder concluded the rape.

So my young lover with his exuberant erotic imagination had only ever known sexual pleasure through bestiality, at puberty, and masturbation after that, until I offered myself to him for the first time. From then on, I was no longer surprised that he returned every day and every night to quench his deep, burning thirst in the secret and obscure spring of my body, to which Islam faithfully paid homage as often as believers, through their prayers, pay homage to their God.

In order for my insatiable lover to perform these five daily pagan prayers, I ensured that the fridge was constantly filled to capacity, especially since, given the close quarters, it was rather small. I didn't skimp on cost: yogurt, cheese, milk, fruit, meat, honey, pastries. This allowed my young lover to sate, in addition to his sexual hunger, another, true hunger, the kind he had known in his childhood, the torturous hunger he told me about one day laughing, the cream from a melting pastry dripping from his full, fresh lips.

Islam's body, svelte as a feline's, began to take on weight, but he remained all muscle, as though he were immune to obesity and any loss of grace. He grew imperceptibly harder and more muscular, silently ripening like a fruit, his proportions adapting like those of a temple erected in accordance with the rules of art, respecting the laws of harmony and a golden ratio. At the sight of his body, of that sculptural beauty, I suddenly thought of the Kom Ombo temple, which takes its name from the village that presented me that beauty. I had spotted this temple overlooking the Nile from afar, during a cruise, a sight that, I now remember, provoked an undefinable feeling inside me. The temple had reddened in the twilight like a blaze.

Watching Islam artistically arrange a basket of fruit set in the middle of the table, I imagined him in that temple, over two thousand years ago, a graceful ephebe chosen by the priests to carry the daily basket of fruit for the sanctuary's two gods, Horus and Sobek.

The scene in my mind prompted me to invent a new name for my young lover, for the ancient ephebe carrying an offering for the gods. The one his devout parents had given him, Islam, clashed both with our life together and with the characteristics I imagined for him. In search of a new name, I whispered to myself: "The ephebe of Kom Ombo," then simply, "Kom Ombo."

Islam was still arranging the basket of fruit when I suddenly called out, "Kom Ombo!"

My abrupt shout made him jump. He turned a slightly worried face toward me and asked, "Did something happen in my village?"

I reassured him and said, "You're Kom Ombo."

"What?"

"From now on, I'm going to call you Kom Ombo."

He burst out laughing: "But I'm not a village…" Then, after brief reflection, he added: "If it makes you happy, call me Kom Ombo, but in that case, you need another name too."

"All right, let me think for a second. But keep arranging the basket of fruit, it might inspire me."

He cheerfully agreed—the inventions of my wild imagination no longer disconcerted him as they had when we first moved in together—and I allowed my gaze to linger on his body, which began to undergo a slow and strange metamorphosis. Would you believe it? This metamorphosis brought on by love, subject to the rigorous laws of the supreme Word, of poetry and song, could only end in a miracle. Within me grew fear and trembling first, then fervor, followed by joy, finally certainty and rapturous contemplation as the temple of Kom Ombo overlooking the Nile, which I had seen redden in the twilight like a blaze, slowly but undeniably descended into the humble bedroom in which I found myself. The gods—Horus, the falcon, and Sobek, the crocodile—deigning to come down from their celestial home, were there in my unworthy apartment, in an empyrean of passion, myth, and transfiguration.

A transfiguration of space, necessary for it to welcome the miracle without shattering into a thousand pieces, but also, and equally imperative, of the gaze and body—mine—so that I could contemplate without risk of blindness and dismemberment the radiant face of the falcon god Horus. Suddenly, the protective transfiguration having momentarily abandoned me, I remembered what the woman from whom I was separated, my dear and unfortunate Mervet, had called me from the very start of our relationship: my falcon!

And for my having committed that insult of ceding to human memory and human pity, the jealous and implacable gods abruptly returned to their heavenly abode and I found myself outside of the enchanted, dazzling sphere of transfiguration.

To think I was about to tell Islam that I had opted for the name of Horus! Oh! I would have borne, and with such pride, the name of the falcon god if my wings hadn't been so awfully trimmed on those fateful days in the month of June 1967, if I had realized what I had been groomed for: to take flight, my wings of steel cutting through the blue sky and colliding with the enemy falcon's wings of identical metal. At this new memory of a defeat that will never cease to rot my soul, I thought of my former companions in arms. It's now been one year since that sweltering month of August when the young swimmers invading the pool forced us to become clumsy, defeated amphibians shamefully returning to shore. Aha! It's not at all the name of the falcon god that suits me but that of the crocodile god, Sobek.

Me, Captain Ni'mat, the god Sobek, the crocodile, the kha-wala*! Penetrated and torn apart by Islam the servant, the god Horus, the falcon, my lover, my master.*

The gods had returned to their empyrean, but their temple was still glowing red, or at least that's how it seemed to me, inside my unworthy apartment.

I stripped completely naked.

A crocodile, I crawled along the ground and said to the falcon youth: "Deign to plant your talons in my back."

He did. It was gentler than when I was a child with an aching back, and my mother would massage me with her palms, spreading a balm over my skin.

I looked to the sky of my shame and my redemption, addressing it, in a whisper, this prayer: "O inscrutable Heaven, be merciful, accept our new names, our names from the bestiary, our innocent names, our sacred names: we are the crocodile and the falcon, ours is a strange and terrible love!"

The Nubian angel, whose ivory-bright skin had abruptly turned purple, translated into Arabic the names of the bird of prey and the amphibian that emblazoned my pagan prayer, which he made his own, chanting the final sequence: "We are Assaqr and Attimsah, ours is a strange and terrible love!"

At that exact moment, the muezzin's call to prayer rang out and coursed into our temple. Perhaps we alone understood its meaning . . .

We had been metamorphosed by raging love, which caused us to lose all memory of our former forms, names, and beliefs, as if all those colossal realities were mere wisps of straw.

Love or tsunami?

Love Tsunami.

IF YOU TWO KHAWALAT DON'T LEAVE THIS NEIGHBORHOOD WE'LL KILL YOU

From a frenzied, ecstatic poetic trance, I plunged into the darkest and most implacable of prose.

History was repeating itself, new inquisitors, the same inquisitors, the eternal inquisitor was again at the threshold of our modest refuge and haven, he had stained the door with his blood letters, we were being tracked, we had become pariahs, but where to run?

This time, Islam felt truly threatened and told me that the wisest thing would be for him to return for a while to his native village—oh my Kom Ombo!—and lie low. I reluctantly agreed, deciding that I myself wouldn't leave Al Fajjala, as the anonymous inquisitor had ordered me to do. I had nothing left to lose and was willing to face any disastrous outcome. Not out of immoderate courage, but simply from lassitude, from disgust for this lethal society that suffocates and annihilates the individual.

My persecutors got what they wanted. They'd shattered my happiness and no longer deemed it necessary that I leave the neighborhood.

All that was left for me was to confront the solitude of my tiny apartment. As I thought, and dreamt, of Kom Ombo...

As I drank.

THREE YEARS *have gone by and the Nubian angel hasn't descended into my hovel again.*

Horus, the falcon god, has forever deserted the sky over my sad home.

Every night, I dream of Kom Ombo's body, of his temple, and I'm awakened by unbearable yearning, eyes filled with tears.

Three years? My body and face, and soul, tell me different-ently every day in the mirror in a scathing refutation of that duration.

Instead, the indifferent and truth-telling mirror shows an aging alcoholic sinking further into decrepitude each day.

In the eyes of the state—how I view that expression with ridicule now, reduced as I am to a pariah—I am officially sixty-five years old.

Three days ago, I "celebrated" that birthday, in the company of an adopted alley cat as decrepit as I am.

I downed two bottles of eau-de-vie, a fire drink supplied by the neighborhood bootlegger who must add God knows what mixtures or poisons. I've just awoken, in a daze, after a dead man's sleep that lasted forty-eight hours. My head is an anvil. I struggle to get up, then fill one glass with a trembling hand, and gulp down the fire drink on an empty stomach. A second glass reinvigorates me, and luckily I still have one bottle left, otherwise how would I tackle this long night ahead of me?

I yearn for the night that never ends.

O sky of Kom Ombo, open up, open up and envelop me in your light, upon a canopy of satin and azure, O temple gods, grant me for the last time the falcon's winged majesty and the crocodile's miry crawl, grant the notes that split and tear my heart and my soul, and then, happy, fulfilled, I will make of myself a basket of fruits, an offering, for you, and all desire in me extinguished, my soul forever pacified, I will finally be able to smile at the serenity calling to me, that has always called to me, O infinite serenity of the eternal night!

Cairo, February 3, 2006

The translator would like to acknowledge Hervé Sanson, Sidney Ola Smith, and Ghada Mourad, whose scholarship on Mohamed Leftah informed this translation.

MOHAMED LEFTAH was a novelist and journalist born in Settat, Morocco, in 1946. He attended engineering school in Paris and then returned in 1972 to Morocco, where he became a literary critic for *Le Matin du Sahara* and *Le Temps du Maroc*. His career as a novelist began with the publication of the critically acclaimed *Demoiselles de Numidie* in 1992, followed by ten more novels over the next nineteen years. *Captain Ni'mat's Last Stand* is his first novel to be published in English. He died of cancer in 2008.

LARA VERGNAUD is the recipient of two PEN/Heim Translation Fund Grants and a French Voices Grand Prize, and has been nominated for the National Translation Award. Her translation of *The Last One* by Fatima Daas was long-listed for the PEN Translation Prize. Other recent translations include *Born of No Woman* by Franck Bouysse and *Trace & Aura* by Patrick Boucheron (co-translated with Willard Wood).